Advice from a father to his son
Don't try to be better than your father, try to be your best self and you will be better than your father.

About the Author

Today, Paul Bisson works as an international consultant for communication projects and part-time university teacher. With a diverse background, he has worked around the globe as a director, producer, a federal official, and even as the director of the Canadian pavilion at various world expositions. After his politically and militarily flavored novel, *Le Castor et le Coq,* he now returns with *Murder at the Golden Apple,* part one of a thrilling detective trilogy.

Murder at the Golden Apple

Paul Bisson

Murder at the Golden Apple

Olympia Publishers
London

www.olympiapublishers.com
OLYMPIA PAPERBACK EDITION

Copyright © Paul Bisson 2024

The right of Paul Bisson to be identified as author of
this work has been asserted in accordance with sections 77 and 78 of
the Copyright, Designs and Patents Act 1988.

All Rights Reserved

No reproduction, copy or transmission of this publication
may be made without written permission.
No paragraph of this publication may be reproduced,
copied or transmitted save with the written permission of the publisher,
or in accordance with the provisions
of the Copyright Act 1956 (as amended).

Any person who commits any unauthorised act in relation to
this publication may be liable to criminal
prosecution and civil claims for damage.

A CIP catalogue record for this title is
available from the British Library.

ISBN: 978-1-80439-964-4

This is a work of fiction.
Names, characters, places and incidents originate from the writer's
imagination. Any resemblance to actual persons, living or dead, is
purely coincidental.

First Published in 2024

Olympia Publishers
Tallis House
2 Tallis Street
London
EC4Y 0AB

Printed in Great Britain

Que cela soit su!

Dedication

To Sébastien and Valérie.

Foreword

According to an unsupported legend, Christopher Columbus discovered Saint Lucia, the pearl of the Caribbean, on December 13, 1492, the day of Saint Lucy. The first known inhabitants of the island were the Arawaks, followed by the Kalinagos.

Nestled between Martinique to the north and Saint Vincent and the Grenadines to the south, Saint Lucia is part of the long chain of volcanic islands stretching from Puerto Rico to Venezuela. From Saint Lucia, on a clear day, one can see Martinique and Saint Vincent and the Grenadines in the distance.

The island, shaped like a mango or almost like a pear, has a total area of six hundred and twenty square kilometers and measures only twelve kilometers by thirty. With its mountains, rugged coastline, lush vegetation, coves and sublime beaches, including some volcanic ones, it is unique among its sister islands in the eastern Caribbean. Due to its geographical location and the ocean currents of the Caribbean, Saint Lucia is often spared from tropical cyclones that hit farther north, around Puerto Rico and the Bahamas. However, in 1780, the entire island was devastated by a major hurricane that killed two hundred people.

The languages spoken are English and Creole. Saint Lucian Creole is similar to Creole spoken on other islands in the Lesser Antilles, such as Guadeloupe, Martinique, and Dominica.

The Dutch, English, and French attempted to establish trading posts on the island during the first half of the seventeenth century but encountered strong opposition from the Caribbean inhabitants. France was the first to establish a colony and sign a treaty with the Kalinagos at the end of the seventeenth century. For the next two centuries, France and England fought for control of the island, with the country changing hands fourteen times. Finally, with the Treaty of Paris, England gained control in 1814. The country became independent on February 22, 1979.

Saint Lucians are proud and welcoming people. Saint Lucia, with two Nobel laureates, has earned the title of the most Nobel-prized country in the world per capita. Economist Arthur Lewis in 1979 and writer and poet Derek Walcott in 1992 were the two recipients of this prestigious award.

Saint Lucia is a volcanic island, and its two volcanic mountains, known as the Gros Piton and the Petit Piton, symbols of the country, give strength and character to the landscape and are part of the UNESCO World Heritage Sites.

The capital of Saint Lucia is Castries. It was ravaged by fire four times, in 1796, 1813, 1927, and 1948.

Chapter 01

Monday, May 2, 2005

The last spring morning rains had stopped sweeping across the island of Saint Lucia, and the sun had just begun its day's work when Amanda was dropped off on the main road. She quickly got out of the minivan and headed toward the driver's window to give him the fare for her ride. She always took public transportation to get to work. The service, although rudimentary, was efficient and economical.

She ran as fast as she could down the slope leading to the inn. Amanda was late; she regretted the long night she had spent in the arms of her new friend. They had met just a month ago, but the night before, she had let herself be seduced, willingly given in to his charm.

The inn's gardener, who was doing his daily tasks, let out a sigh of exasperation as he momentarily turned around to watch her pass by. Amanda ignored him.

"Good morning, JJ. I'm sorry for being late," Amanda said, rushing into the inn's vestibule before continuing her run quickly toward the back.

She put on her housekeeping uniform and immediately went back to see JJ at the front desk. Josephine Johnson was the manager of the *Golden Apple Inn*. She was simply called JJ. It was somewhat masculine as a nickname, but Josephine liked the authority it conveyed. She was a woman in her forties, very active in her community. She always paid particular attention to the way she dressed and how she wore her makeup. Josephine was a pretty woman who exuded femininity. She had been managing the establishment alone for ten years and was the absolute boss.

"I'm sorry, JJ," Amanda repeated.

"It's okay, Amanda! Here's the list of rooms to clean, and don't forget that today we're removing all the bedding. It's laundry day."

"Thank you," said the young woman, taking the piece of paper handed to her.

Amanda, along with her colleague Julietta, was assigned to housekeeping duties at the inn, where she had been working since completing her college course a year earlier. She was currently enrolled in a distance education program with an American university to obtain a bachelor's degree in administration. Tall and sporty, which gave her a slightly boyish look, Amanda always wore a big beautiful smile on her face. Her boldness had helped her a lot in her adolescence, but now she was desperately trying tone it down and appear more feminine.

She headed toward room 11, located on the ground floor. As usual, she knocked loudly on the door three times to make sure the occupant wasn't there. With the help of her master key, she opened the door and brought in her housekeeping cart. All the lights were on, and the bed had not been used. *Weird*, she thought. As she headed toward the bathroom, which was a bit further back, she let out a loud scream of terror.

"JJ, JJ, my God! There's a man lying on the floor," she said, running toward the front desk.

***

Two hours had passed before the police authorities of Castries finally arrived at the inn. JJ and Amanda had not returned to the room since the discovery. Hercule Simpson, the chief of police, accompanied by his deputy, Danny Ford, immediately headed toward the two women who seemed frozen in place.

"Who discovered the victim?" he asked.

"Me," said Amanda timidly, raising her hand slightly.

"Describe to us the circumstances under which it all happened," demanded the chief of police.

The small front hall that served as a reception area had a counter and two armchairs. Hercule Simpson liked to take control of any room he entered by a show of strength and dominance as was the case at that moment. The restricted space, occupied by the presence of the four people, created an intimidating atmosphere for the two women. Nevertheless, Amanda recounted the beginning of her workday until the moment she had seen the body lying on the floor in room 11.

"Please take us to the room," ordered the chief of police authoritatively.

Hercule Simpson had been the chief of police in Castries for over twenty-five years. He ruled as king and master in Castries and throughout the country, as his title conferred on him the rank of commander of the entire Saint Lucia police forces. The greater Castries, the capital of Saint Lucia, encompassed over eighty per cent of the country's population.

Standing over six feet tall, still athletic despite his advanced age and graying hair, he exuded a fully assumed sheriff's authority.

They entered room 11. As Amanda had explained, the

victim lay on the floor, face down, just outside the bathroom. His feet were in the doorway, and his pants and underpants were pulled down to his knees. A small pool of blood, that had congealed on the hard ceramic floor came from the victim's head. The chief of police, who seemed to be on guard, immediately noticed the scar on the victim's forehead, likely caused by a blunt object.

The victim, a black man over six feet tall, had a slender, athletic build. He was probably in his early twenties.

"Can you confirm," Simpson asked Amanda, "that the scene is the same as when you entered this morning?"

"Yes!"

"And that no one has entered this room since the discovery?" he asked, addressing both women this time.

They confirmed with a nod of their heads as the deputy began to capture the scene with his camera. The chief bent down to check the victim's pulse by placing two fingers on his carotid artery. He did the same on the wrist.

"Nobody move!" he suddenly ordered.

Amanda and JJ looked at him, stunned.

"The murderer is still in the room," he continued.

Turning to his deputy, he ordered him to escort the two women out quietly. They did not need to be asked twice and left with a frightened look on their faces.

Once the women were out, the chief pulled up the victim's pants and pointed out the bite marks on his right ankle to his deputy. He then ordered him to notify the chief coroner and to call Willie.

The deputy did as he was told. Danny Ford, a man of average height, had joined the police force after a career as an international cricket player on the West Indies team. He had already worn the colors of the Saint Lucia national team that played in the Caribbean Premier League of cricket. In the years that followed, he had given up all sports activities, which had caused him to gain weight. He was now a little overweight and bald.

Willie arrived first. In his early forties, with a Harry-style haircut from the Three Stooges, he was a stout little man with a pragmatic look on life. He was wearing a khaki brown safari-style outfit and proudly displayed two reptile tattoos on his forearms. He held a four-cubic-foot transport box in one hand and an instrument in the other. The police chief immediately guided him to room 11. Willie already knew the reason for his presence at the inn.

Outside, the gardener curiously watched the scene through the window of room 11, pretending to prune an adjacent floral bush. He tried to position himself to see the corpse while snipping in the air. Hercule noticed his behavior.

"Did you spot him?" Willie asked the police chief.

"No," he replied.

Willie set down his box and headed for the bathroom. He gave an indifferent glance at the victim's body, walked around it, and holding his capture tool firmly, took a quick peek into the bathroom.

"Here it is, still looking for the moistest spot," he said confidently.

The fer-de-lance was coiled defensively behind the toilet bowl. For this reptile, the best defense was offense. The trigonocéphale was a species of snake from the Viperidae family, called fer-de-lance or Kravat in Creole. The word Kravat came from the French word 'cravate' because from head to tail, it had the shape of a knotted tie. It was found only in the

West Indies, mainly in Martinique and Saint Lucia. Its venom was deadly if not treated within four to six hours of the bite.

Willie extended his arm toward the beast, still holding his capture instrument, a long-handled pair of tongs.

"Wait, let me take a picture," Danny interjected.

He quickly complied, and Willie resumed his position. He confidently extended his arm, seeking to avoid the fer-de-lance's gaze, knowing its power of hypnosis. With a precise movement, he closed the instrument around the snake. He headed for his box while the trigonocéphale writhed in an attempt to escape the tongs. Eventually, he placed it in the box and closed it so the reptile could not escape.

"Well done," summarized Police Chief Simpson. "You know what to do now."

"Yes," he replied, leaving the room with his catch.

Meanwhile, Albert Monfils arrived on the scene. A doctor by profession, Albert had been the chief coroner of Saint Lucia for over twenty years. An elegant man in his late fifties, he was dressed in a navy-blue Armani stretch suit, silk tie, and Italian leather shoes. He always had a white handkerchief in his hand to wipe his forehead due to his attire and the Caribbean heat.

Police Chief Simpson and Albert Monfils knew each other well. His presence at the crime scene was justified by the fact that the cause of death was unknown, as was the identity of the deceased person, which the authorities would have to discover. The police chief preferred to wait for his arrival before handling the victim's wallet and passport.

As Willie left and the coroner entered room 11, Danny pointed out the bloodstained towel hook in the bathroom to his boss.

"Hello, Albert, thank you for coming," Hercule greeted

him.

"It's my job," Albert replied. "Tell me the facts before I begin my analysis."

Meanwhile, JJ sent a text overseas to the owner of the *Golden Apple Inn*.

The *Golden Apple Inn* had been built by the current owner, Nigel Glenwood, about twenty years earlier on a one-acre plot of land in the Marisule neighborhood that his father had granted him. Nigel's father had inherited a large plot of land that stretched from the main road to the Caribbean Sea, with a seafront of two thousand feet and an area of twenty-five acres.

The *Golden Apple* was an endemic fruit tree of Saint Lucia. Its shape resembled that of a pear, and its fruit was similar to an apple with a skin like a kiwi and a brownish-golden color. The fruit had a slightly bitter taste, especially on the first bite. Locally, this fruit was used to make a strong eau-de-vie, like a German schnapps. It was Nigel's mother's favorite fruit.

The inn had twenty-five rooms, with the upper floor rooms featuring a balcony and the ground floor rooms a stone patio. All offered a superb view of the Caribbean Sea and the entrance to the port of Castries.

This neighborhood, called Marisule, was located halfway between Castries, the capital, and Rodney Bay, the main tourist area of Saint Lucia. Nigel's father had once owned almost the entire Marisule neighborhood. He and his father before him had run a large and prosperous chicken farm on the flat part of the estate at the bottom of the slope, about a hundred feet from the water's edge.

Nigel Glenwood, born in Saint Lucia about forty years earlier, had been living in Great Britain for about fifteen years. Nigel was known and adored throughout the West Indies and was the pride of Saint Lucia. He was recognized as the best cricket player of all time from the West Indies.

He, Danny Ford, and the late Charlie Liverpool were nicknamed the fer de lance trio of Saint Lucia on the West Indies cricket team. Together, they had greatly contributed to the two victories of the West Indies team in the Cricket World Cup, including the memorable one against England.

Nigel immediately called Josephine upon receiving the text. It was almost eleven o'clock in Saint Lucia when she answered the call while it was four p.m., in London. JJ provided a recap of the dramatic event of the morning. She tried to remain calm on the phone, but her voice betrayed apparent nervousness.

"Has his death been confirmed?" he asked eagerly.

"Yes and no, I don't know, the chief coroner is in the room right now," JJ nervously replied.

"Is the police chief still there?"

"Yes, Mr. Simpson is still here with his deputy."

"Who is this lodger? What do you know about him?"

"He's a young man, early twenties. He arrived two weeks ago without giving a departure date. He was rather discreet. He had dual citizenship, British and Saint Lucian. He registered under the name James Charles Liverpool, but the name on his British passport and Saint Lucian citizenship card is James Charles."

"What was he doing on the island?" Nigel asked.

"Most of the time, he left the inn in the late morning and returned in the late afternoon. Julietta would know more than me, she often chatted with him."

"Despite the time difference, please call me, as soon as the police chief and coroner leave the scene," Nigel asked.

"Yes, without fail, Mr. Glenwood," JJ replied.

The chief coroner completed his analysis. Albert Monfils confirmed the death but could not establish the exact cause and circumstances. Was it the deadly bite on the ankle or the blow to the forehead that had been the determining factor? He estimated that the death had occurred around three o'clock the previous night. He finished his analysis after talking to JJ and examining the register of the *Golden Apple Inn* in order to properly identify the victim.

"I will need the opinion of the medical examiner at the morgue to complete my report," he said to the police chief.

"For my part, the scenario is quite simple," said Simpson.

"A fer-de-lance snake entered his room and hid behind the toilet. The roommate went to the bathroom, sat on the toilet, and the snake attacked at ankle height. The victim, surprised by the bite, fell forward and hit his forehead on the lingerie hook. He staggered to the door and, losing consciousness, fell to the floor at the exit of the bathroom. The venom took effect before he could regain his senses, and he died of poisoning."

"Your scenario is probable, but I will still wait for the opinion of the medical examiner before completing my report," the chief coroner replied. "And make sure to take fingerprints everywhere in the room and on the doors and windows of access," he added.

The coroner contacted the morgue to come and collect the body, then left with the victim's personal documents.

Police Chief Simpson went to see JJ at the reception. Amanda was with her.

"You two will have to come with me to the police station so that we can take your statement," Simpson said.

"It's impossible for me to leave the inn," JJ immediately

replied.

"What does that mean… A statement?" asked Amanda.

"We need to question you and obtain all the necessary information to conclude the investigation," Simpson replied. "As for you, Josephine, I will ask my deputy to take your statement right here."

Hercule Simpson left the inn with Amanda heading to downtown Castries.

***

London, England
Eight P.M., The Same Day

The coroner eventually obtained a transcontinental telephone line.

"Good evening!"

"Mrs. Charles, Jessica Charles?"

"Yes. Who am I speaking to?"

"Good evening, my name is Albert Monfils and I am the chief coroner of Saint Lucia."

"No, no, no… Don't tell me something has happened to my son!"

"Mrs. Charles, I regret to inform you of the death of James Charles…"

"No… Don't tell me that… What happened to my son?"

"I'm sorry; I would like to offer my sincere condolences. I can assure you that the government of Saint Lucia takes this incident seriously and we will do everything we can to solve this tragedy. For now…"

"I told him not to go… It's my fault…"

"I reiterate that we take this event very seriously," said Albert. "We are at the beginning of the investigation, but I wanted to share with you the known facts…"

Albert Monfils explained to her the main points of his report and asked her if she intended to come to Saint Lucia.

"Of course, I will come, but when, I don't know, I need to think," she replied.

"May I ask if you know anyone on the island who could come to the morgue to identify your son?" asked coroner Monfils.

"No, no one on the island knew about the existence of my son, at least as far as I know," she answered.

"Please, let me know your intentions as soon as possible," said the coroner. "I will be able to contact you again after the medical examiner's analysis at the morgue."

Jessica Charles was forty-two years old. She had left Saint Lucia secretly in her early twenties to settle in London, England. At that time, she had just won the Miss West Indies contest. A few weeks after her coronation, due to persistent nausea, she had consulted a doctor in Castries who had informed her that she was one month and one week pregnant. She had asked him to keep this information secret and, after careful consideration, had decided to leave her native country, leaving her parents in ignorance.

In England, she had opened a hair and spa boutique. Her mother had a hair salon in Castries and had passed on to her the basics of hairdressing and her entrepreneurial knowledge. Her beauty, charm, charisma, and intelligence had enabled her to achieve success. Her business, called Le Spa, had a prominent location in the Kensington district. Proud of her success, she had been able to open a second boutique in downtown London, in the city. For her, the well-being and education of her son remained paramount.

***

The afternoon was drawing to a close, and the sun had begun its slow descent off the coast of the island. Only the huge cruise ships leaving the port of Castries cast shadows on the natural and sublime sunset like big clouds. The reflection on the facade of the inn highlighted the Caribbean cotton candy pink color of its exterior. The inn was well surrounded by three small gardens, each different from the others.

The left one contained large fruit trees, with the largest one, called the breadfruit tree, spreading like an umbrella over the others. There were also apricot trees from the Caribbean, two mango trees, a weeping fig tree, and, on the periphery, needing a more direct reception of sunlight, the golden apples.

In front of the inn, lining a gentle slope leading to the Caribbean Sea, one could see small flowering shrubs and cacti framed on each side by a row of miniature palm trees. Hibiscus, oleanders, ixoras, and yellow allamandas took full advantage of the sunlight.

The right garden exclusively hosted banana trees. Dessert bananas with sweet flesh, cooking bananas rich in starch, short bananas, and small green bananas coexisted in this restricted space of fifty square meters.

JJ was trying to keep calm, but the death of a person in her inn troubled her greatly. She decided to go outside, to the gardens, to regain her composure and reflect on what had happened.

"What a day!" JJ exclaimed to the inn's gardener.

"Impossible, impossible," he muttered repeatedly.

"What's impossible?" she asked him.

"Kravat… Impossible!" he replied as he walked away to continue his work.

As he was leaving, JJ mentioned to him that his gardens were sublime and that Mr. Glenwood would be very pleased with him. He shrugged at the comment. He had been the gardener since the very beginning of the inn's operations. In fact, he had proposed a landscaping plan for the new inn. Once it had been accepted, he had set to work on its implementation.

Josephine knew the gardener well and didn't pay any attention to his indifference. She decided to return to her duties.

"What should I do about room 11?" Amanda asked JJ as she entered the inn.

"I'm sorry, the coroner has requested that we not touch anything until further notice; however, the chief of police told me that all the information for the investigation has been collected and we can proceed with the clean-up," JJ replied.

"So?"

"Wait, I need to talk to Nigel and I will ask him to decide," JJ responded.

"Okay."

***

The next day, Tuesday, May 3
Quebec City, Quebec

A man in his fifties was about to prepare his daily martini when the phone rang in his kitchen.

"Hello! Mr. Maximilien Le Gardeur?"

"Maximilien Le Gardeur here. Who am I speaking to?"

"Mon nom... My name is Jessica Charles... A mutual acquaintance told me about you."

"Oh yes! Hopefully in a good way," he replied teasingly.

The caller had a pleasant voice with a sensual tone. Maximilien had recently signed up on a dating website, so he initially thought the call was related to his search for a soulmate. However, the international area code indicated that the call was from overseas.

"Mr. Le Gardeur, I need your services."

"My services?" he repeated cautiously.

"My son died under suspicious circumstances yesterday in Saint Lucia, and I do not trust the local authorities."

"Allow me first to offer you my condolences, madam."

Maximilien Le Gardeur, known as Max to his close friends, had been a fighter pilot for the Canadian military where he had earned a solid reputation. During his time stationed in Baden Baden, he was nicknamed the Canadian Top Gun. He had obtained his pilot and civil engineering degrees from the military academy in Kingston.

Jessica explained to Maximilien the circumstances surrounding her son's death based on the information obtained from the chief coroner. She emphasized her distrust of the local police and mentioned that her son's presence in his grandparents' country might have been viewed unfavorably by certain individuals. Maximilien wanted to know why her son had traveled to Saint Lucia. Jessica was vague in her response, but she mentioned that he wanted to explore his parents' homeland, learn more about his biological father's death, and that she had received no news from him since he left.

"Seriously, Mrs. Charles, I do not see how I could be of

assistance. In fact, I do not understand why you were advised to contact me."

"I was told that you are an excellent investigator," she replied. "Apparently, you have successfully solved international dramas with efficiency and tact."

For the past fifteen years, Maximilien had been working for NATO, conducting multilateral investigations among its member countries into actions or events that could potentially undermine their collective security and defense obligations.

His successes had been recognized, and his reputation as an investigator had spread to other organizations such as the UN and the Canadian and American intelligence services. He had occasionally been hired by these organizations to investigate political–military issues. Even INTERPOL had enlisted his services to solve international political-military assassinations.

"Please, don't make me beg you," she pleaded with him.

"I'm sorry, Madame Charles, but I am not your man," he replied firmly.

"I have the financial means to pay you, all your expenses will be reimbursed, your price will be mine," Jessica insisted.

"I regret it, and I wish you good luck," he said in a firm tone.

"I sincerely thought you would have been sympathetic to my request, considering what you have experienced with your own son," Jessica said, desperate.

This last comment struck Maximilien like a bolt of lightning. On her part, Jessica already regretted her boldness.

"Good evening and good luck, madame," he said before ending the conversation.

That evening, Maximilien treated himself to a few martinis. His thoughts wandered from one past event to another. There had been the divorce from the mother of his children, the distancing of his daughter, the death of his father, but it was the incident involving his son Eric that dominated his thoughts.

Maximilien Le Gardeur's career change had actually been provoked by a dramatic event. His son, who was twenty years old at the time, was going through a difficult period and was involved with a street gang. One day, he became involved in an illegal transaction in Puerto Vallarta, Mexico, and was shot and killed. As soon as he heard the news of his son's death, Maximilien, distraught, left Canada for Mexico.

On the scene, after reviewing the investigation report that outrageously incriminated his son, he decided to conduct his own investigation. The report identified his son as the aggressor and indicated that his killer had acted in self-defence. This did not match his image of his son at all, even though he knew he willingly participated in such transactions.

He teamed up with one of the investigators on the ground and, after two weeks of interrogations, risky meetings, he managed to shed a different light on the outcome of the tragedy. His son was no longer seen as the aggressor, but as the victim of a ruthless individual. A small consolation, but it helped him come to terms with this enormous loss in his life. He brought his son's body back to Canada for a respectful funeral.

He was finishing his third martini as he walked down the hallway to his room. He stopped in front of a photo of his son, taken a few months before the unfortunate incident. Overcome by emotion, he decided to return to the kitchen. He picked up the phone and dialed the last received call.

"Madame Charles, I am willing to try to help you."

"Thank you, Mr. Le Gardeur."

A long conversation followed.

Chapter 02

Wednesday, May 4, 2005

Willie Norris was feeding his tenants.

"You seem hungry today," he said to them as he fed them.

Willie went from one glass cage to another, carefully serving their weekly ration. Occasionally, he felt a momentary shiver of unease run through him, as if one of the creatures could suddenly appear out of nowhere and surprise him with a deadly bite.

He worked at the Saint Lucia Reptile Preservation Agency, which was established in the 1980s after Saint Lucia gained independence, to prevent the extinction of certain reptile species unique to the island. Three species, in particular, were part of this program: the St. Lucia Whiptail, the Anolis luciae lizard of the Dactyloidae family, known for its multi-colored colors, and the St. Lucia racer snake, Liophis ornatus, the rarest non-venomous snake in the world. According to the latest census, there were only eighteen left on the island.

What had almost caused their extinction was the mongoose, a formidable predator for snakes, which was introduced to the island in the late 19th century to eliminate venomous snakes. The species they wanted to control was the fer de lance viper, but their favorite prey was the St. Lucia racer snake.

To prevent the extinction of the St. Lucia racer snake, like the Anolis luciae lizard, they were captured and released on a small island about a kilometer from Saint Lucia called Maria. The place was inaccessible to mongooses. Willie had participated in this initiative with pride.

Suddenly, the phone at the agency rang. Willie picked up the receiver. It was Chief of Police Hercule Simpson on the other end.

"Understood," Willie simply said after the chief gave his instructions.

Willie carried out his tasks in a simple and orderly manner. He had no choice, as an error on his part could cost him his life. His agency office was located inland on the mountainside of the island. It was a former French garrison building from the early 1800s, refurbished to house the Saint Lucian conservation agency.

***

The coroner was reading the report from the medical examiner at the morgue. The doctor confirmed the time of death and that the venomous bite was indeed the cause of death. The blow to the head, regardless of what caused it, could not have resulted in the victim's death. The victim's blood alcohol level was minimal, and no traces of any drugs were identified in his system. The report also confirmed that a sample of cells had been taken from the victim for DNA testing.

Albert Monfils picked up the phone and called the police headquarters in Castries. He asked to speak to Hercule Simpson. He was put on hold for five minutes before the call was transferred to the chief's office.

"Hello, Mr. Coroner. I apologize for the delay, I was…"

"It's all right, Hercule, there's no need to be formal. I'm

calling to share with you the main points of the medical examiner's report regarding James Charles. Your deductions about the crime scene have been corroborated."

"Who said anything about a crime?" replied Hercule. "It's more of a fatal incident, an unfortunate encounter with a fer de lance viper."

"Regardless, I rely on you to further elaborate on your investigation report. Have you taken all the necessary depositions?" he asked.

"I've done my job," Simpson replied impatiently.

"I hope so, because the victim's mother will be here in two days. You know James Charles' mother, I presume…"

"Not to my knowledge, why?"

"Like you, she was often in the company of the West Indies cricket team that won the World Cup a little over twenty years ago. That's what she told me during our second conversation."

"I don't remember, it's possible," the chief quickly interjected before continuing to discuss other necessary police measures to conclude the investigation.

Albert took the opportunity to inform him that Mrs. Charles had hired an internationally renowned investigator to analyze the cause and exact circumstances surrounding the death of the victim in room 11.

"What's the name of this investigator?" Simpson asked eagerly.

"Maximilien Le Gardeur, a former major in the Canadian Armed Forces. Do you know him?"

"The name doesn't ring a bell."

"He'll be here tomorrow. I'm counting on you to provide him with all the necessary support for his own investigation."

Albert continued with an authoritative tone, making sure

his recommendation would not be perceived as a request, but as an obligation.

***

Thursday, May 5, 2005

In the early afternoon, Max Le Gardeur was aboard flight AC1050 from Toronto to Vieux Fort. The flight would last for five hours. Saint Lucia International Airport was located in Vieux Fort, in the southern part of the island, while the *Golden Apple Inn* was located in the northern part. Max had decided to stay at the inn for the duration of his investigation.

"Dear passengers, this is your captain speaking," Max suddenly heard. "In a few minutes, we will be flying over the island of Saint Lucia before distancing ourselves to prepare for landing. At that time, I will invite you to take a look through the left windows to catch a glimpse of the two Piton volcanoes. You won't be disappointed. I take this opportunity to thank you for choosing to fly with Air Canada and have a pleasant stay in Saint Lucia!"

Max happened to be on the left side, in the aisle seat. He glanced at the window and noticed that the window shade was halfway open. He looked at his neighbor for a moment, who immediately understood his request.

"Thank you. Is this your first trip to Saint Lucia?" Max asked.

"No. Ah, there they are," the man replied, leaning back to give him enough space to observe the scenery.

Indeed, it was worth the look: two twin cones, one larger than the other, almost perfectly asymmetrical, with their sides plunging into the Caribbean Sea. Their imposing presence dominated the entire geographical landscape of the island.

"Truly spectacular!" exclaimed Max.

"Yes, indeed. You can climb the larger one if you're interested."

They continued their discussion until the moment of landing and the complete stop of the aircraft. Maximilien took advantage of the time to learn more about the island.

As soon as Max stepped off the plane and descended onto the tarmac via the aircraft stairs, he immediately felt the tropical heat. Yellow arrows on the asphalt guided passengers toward the customs hangar for arrivals. Already, after a few steps on the tarmac, he was sweating profusely in his long pants, compression socks, shirt, and undershirt.

The airport, somewhat run-down, seemed to be well managed. Customs clearance would likely be expedited. On his customs declaration form, completed during the flight, Max had indicated: Canadian, single, tourist visit, fourteen-day stay, return on Thursday, May 19—he had agreed with Mrs. Charles on a two-week stay while knowing he could modify his return flight depending on the outcome of his investigation—and declared a box of 25 Romeo & Julietta Number Four cigars worth five hundred Canadian dollars in his checked luggage.

"Your first visit to Saint Lucia?" the customs officer asked him as she reviewed his documents.

"Yes."

"Welcome to my country," she said, stamping his passport and declaration form.

"Thank you," Max replied, offering her a smile.

According to his research, after retrieving his luggage, he could take a taxi to Marisule for seventy-five US dollars. As he was leaving the customs area, he heard his name called several times. He turned and saw a man in police uniform holding a sign that read: Maximilien Le Gardeur.

"Monsieur Maximilien Le Gardeur?"

"Yes!"

"Welcome to Saint Lucia, I'm Peter Monrose. It's an honor for me to meet you. Let me take your luggage, I'll take you to your hotel."

Maximilien nodded. He quickly felt that he could trust this individual. Once on the main road toward the Atlantic side, Peter began to explain to Maximilien the task that had been assigned to him by command. Peter assured Maximilien that he was at his service to facilitate his investigation, movements, and research.

Max listened attentively while examining his new accomplice. In his early thirties, tall, speaking with ease, well-groomed, handsome with a genuine smile, he exuded the necessary confidence to carry out his job. Maximilien had the extraordinary gift for perceiving the truth, for assessing the level of nervousness in his interlocutors. He was a walking lie detector. He also had a great ability to adapt, quickly grasping how the circumstances of a situation could have developed and in what context.

This had greatly helped him in his international investigations with NATO and the UN. Especially, during a mission in Ukraine as part of a military principles agreement between NATO and Ukraine to establish a peace partnership, Major Le Gardeur had to analyze the state of the Ukrainian forces and assess their level of loyalty to the agreement. The paradox was that Ukraine had already signed a military partnership with Russia. Ukraine possessed the third largest military power in Europe after France and Russia.

He had the opportunity to meet with high-ranking officers and some senior officials. He titled his report *CAUTION*. He felt that Ukraine was playing on two fronts and that the roots of the Moscow Empire were still dominant, both politically and militarily, but also within the Ukrainian intelligentsia. The report was shared with the European Union, which concluded an association agreement with Ukraine to facilitate free trade.

As Peter described each village and plot of land along the road, Max decided to interrupt him.

"So, where should we start?" Max inquired.

"Start with what?" Peter responded, clearly surprised.

"The investigation, the reason for my presence here," Max explained.

"But... you're the great investigator," Peter stammered, losing some of his confidence.

"Peter, what would you do in my place? What would be the first steps to take?" Max asked.

"Well, I suppose we would need to visit the scene of the crime, read the investigation and coroner's reports, and interrogate the key players," Peter suggested.

"Exactly. We'll start tomorrow, first thing in the morning. For now, resume your role as tour guide."

The journey took an hour and a half, mostly due to the rush hour traffic in downtown Castries. Marisule was a dormitory neighborhood located further north of Castries. Upon arrival, Max was greeted by Josephine Jackson and her assistant, a man named Charlie, who were waiting for them in the inn's parking lot. The entire staff had been informed of the reason for Max's stay at the inn.

"Welcome to the *Golden Apple*. I hope your flight was

pleasant," JJ greeted him as soon as he stepped out of the car.

"Very well, thank you, Mrs. Jackson," Max replied, recognizing her voice.

"Please, call me JJ. Everyone knows me by that nickname. I've prepared room 12 for you, as you requested."

"Perfect," he responded, while Charlie retrieved his suitcase from the trunk of the car.

"Dinner will be served in an hour. Does that suit you?" JJ asked.

"Only if it comes with a gin and tonic as an aperitif," Max replied.

"No problem. Please follow me for check-in. Charlie will take care of bringing your suitcase to your room."

Max nodded in agreement and turned to Peter to reiterate their meeting point, right here at the inn, the next day at nine o'clock.

***

Friday, May 6, 2005

Room 12 was the last one on the ground floor. Max had managed to have a decent night's sleep thanks to his pillow. Before every trip, he made sure to pack his pillow in his luggage. Over the course of his many business travels, he had quickly realized that sleeping with his own pillow provided an unconscious, almost hypnotic sense of security that facilitated his sleep; it was like a security blanket for a young child. It wasn't something he shared with others; in fact, his first instinct in the morning was to put it back in his suitcase before the housekeeping staff came through.

Around eight-thirty, he headed to the dining room for breakfast. The room, open to the outside, was adjacent to the reception area and overlooked the garden of large fruit trees, which offered no view of the sea. The morning breeze came and went as it pleased. A mixture of spicy cooking smells and the sweet fragrance of tropical fruits filled the room. He was greeted by Annetta, the inn's cook.

"Good morning, Mr. Le Gardeur!"

"Good morning, madam."

"Did you have a good night?" she asked him.

"Reasonable, I would say, despite the barking of dogs during the evening, the continuous musical backdrop of crickets throughout the night, and the chorus of all the neighborhood roosters at dawn."

Annetta laughed at his comment. They got to know each other. Max guessed she was about fifty years old. Wearing a Caribbean headscarf, she was petite, but her stride was strong and confident. As the inn's cook, she lived in the neighborhood and offered catering services, mainly for desserts, from her own home. Her specialty was wedding cakes.

She knew the reason for Max's stay on the island and brought it up right away.

"Poor little thing, he was so handsome and polite. It's strange, this tragedy. They say the mother is supposed to arrive in the next few days to organize the funeral right here in Saint Lucia," she said, looking for confirmation from the investigator.

"Yes, indeed. She was born in Saint Lucia. Did you know that?"

"Yes and no. You know, ever since the young man's death, there have been a lot of rumors and gossip circulating in town."

"You saw him every day for breakfast and dinner?" Max

asked.

"Yes, except Sundays, my day off. He always sat at the same table."

"What do you know about him?"

"To be honest, our conversations were limited to the weather. Sometimes he would ask me for directions to a particular place. Julietta would know more, I often saw them talking together."

"Who is Julietta?" Max inquired.

"She's one of the housekeeping staff here at the inn."

Maximilien mentioned to her that he would have to interview all the inn's staff, but only after reviewing the various reports completed after the discovery of the body.

"For now, I'm hungry," he declared. "What do you have for me?"

"I'll prepare a plate with two eggs, some cold meats, an assortment of fruits, and some bake."

"Bake?"

"Yes, it's a specialty of the Caribbean, it's like a fritter, you'll see, it's delicious. Take a seat at one of the tables; I'll bring you some coffee."

At exactly nine o'clock, Peter Monrose arrived at the inn. Immediately, Max asked JJ to give him access to room 11. To his disappointment, he found that the room had been cleaned and prepared for the next occupant. JJ explained that she had received conflicting instructions from the chief of police and the chief coroner regarding the crime scene, and the owner had ordered them to follow the instructions of the chief of police.

"This is extremely disappointing," Max said aloud, looking thoughtful. "Peter, there's nothing left to do here for now. Let's go to the police station to review the reports."

"Okay," Peter replied immediately.

"Madame Jackson, I would like—"

"Please, call me JJ," she interrupted with a smile.

"This afternoon, I would like to be able to interview all the staff members who worked at the inn since the victim's arrival. Is that possible?"

"Yes, but Annetta, the cook, doesn't restart her day until five o'clock. I could ask her to come in earlier."

"Perfect, we will interview her last. In the meantime, I would ask you to prepare a list of all the staff members involved and indicate their roles and regular working hours."

Peter and Max set off for the police station. It took about twenty minutes to drive from Marisule to Castries, but since there was only one road that could be taken, it was always difficult to predict the duration of the journey.

The building that housed the Castries police station dated back to the 1890s and had been built by the British. Between 1885 and 1900, the British had erected several military and administrative buildings on the island of Saint Lucia. The newly independent government of Saint Lucia had restored them all for its own administrative and legal needs.

The one assigned to the police station was formerly the Married Women's Quarters, which was used to house and protect the wives of officers during times of war.

All these three-story buildings had the same architectural signature—walls of eighteen-inch-thick yellow bricks, which now had a marbled yellow, brownish, and charred appearance due to oxidation and the sea air, giving them an old-fashioned but pleasant look—a system of round columns and decorative green wrought-iron beams for the balconies and other supports, and a metal roof. A medieval-style brick arcade mural formed the facade of the galleries on the first floor. The finishing woodwork had been completed using various local wood species.

Peter retrieved all the documents, and Maximilien and he settled in the police station's meeting room. They allowed themselves an hour to read.

Max pushed the documents aside and turned thoughtfully to look out the small window at the port of Castries. Peter paused his reading to hear Maximilien Le Gardeur's first comments.

"The coroner's report is informative, but the police investigation report is one-sided," he began.

Peter did not reply, choosing to wait for Max's next words. Max had shared with Peter all the information he had obtained from the victim's mother before leaving Quebec. The same information she had given to her son.

"Let's take stock, if you don't mind, my friend Peter."

They began to assess the situation. A young man, James Charles, twenty years old, born in England to a Saint Lucian mother, Jessica Charles, forty-four years old, who had left her home country while pregnant to settle abroad, decides, on the brink of his twentieth birthday, to visit the land of his parents and grandparents, to uncover the truth about his father's accidental death. He arrives, presumably moving around, trying to meet people, his family, questioning people, perhaps causing some disturbance. And then, after two weeks, on a Sunday, while he is in his room at the inn, a venomous snake that had slithered in bites him fatally. Startled, he reflexively lurches forward, banging his head hard against the towel hook. He loses consciousness as the venom takes its toll.

***

London, England
One Year Earlier, 2004

James Charles, on the eve of his nineteenth birthday, had just completed an exam at the Faculty of Law of King's College London. It was almost noon. Instead of going home, he decided to go to his mother's shop in the city center. Along the way, he sent her a text: "Hi, Mom, on my way, would like to continue our conversation from this morning, don't make any lunch plans. See you soon."

Dressed in the dress code of his university, stylishly preppy, he exuded confidence and pride in his academic achievements.

As he emerged from the nearest subway station to the shop, he realized his mother hadn't responded to his text. He picked up his pace, not wanting her to leave her office early, pretending to have a business lunch. Indeed, as he reached the entrance of the shop, she was about to step out onto the street.

"What timing! You were coming to meet me, I suppose?" he said sarcastically.

"Hi, Charles, I already had a meeting scheduled," she replied.

"Well, then, come on, I'll walk you back to your office so you can cancel it," he said, gallantly taking her arm.

She offered no resistance and had no need to cancel anything. James was eager to continue the conversation about his origins, about his family in the Caribbean.

Jessica Charles had always stuck to the same story with her son regarding the reasons for her departure from Saint Lucia and why she had never disclosed his birth to her parents.

"I made a mistake, and I didn't want my parents to suffer because of it," she had told him. "There, being pregnant and unmarried is perceived as the ultimate taboo. Especially for my parents and their relatives. If you only knew how difficult it was for them to accept that I entered as a candidate for Miss West Indies. Every year, I send them a Christmas card to say hello, assure them of my well-being, without revealing my location, without them knowing of your existence. Your father died as a result of a tragic event that occurred a month before I made the decision to leave. I don't want to tell you more; I would like you to respect that. I offer you a safe environment and a good education."

"This is your story, now I want to know mine, the truth," James said when his mother gave him the same explanation that day. "I want to know my grandparents and my father's family. I want to know the country of my roots. I want to know more about my father's death," he concluded fervently, struggling to hold back his tears.

Both of them started to cry. James, while fighting his sobs, told her that he would go to Saint Lucia after his second-year exams, the following year.

"My decision is made. If you don't want to tell me more before I leave, I will go to the archives office when I'm there and knock on every door until I find my grandparents," he said in a trembling voice.

"You will create a shock among my family. Please, don't do this," his mother pleaded with him.

"I'm going anyway, and I expect you to entrust me with more information about my origins. Your cooperation would be appreciated," he added with a hint of authority.

She sank into her chair, looking at her beloved son while

reflecting on what she was about to reveal to him.

***

Back at the police station, Peter and Max continued their discussion.

"I would like to have a brief initial interview with the chief of police before we return to the inn. Can you check with him?" Max asked Peter.

"Let me check, I'll be right back," he replied, leaving the room.

Peter returned immediately, mentioning that they could have fifteen minutes with him today around eleven forty-five.

"Perfect, in the meantime, let's think together. The cause and circumstances of death may be true, but what about the two weeks leading up to it? I think the answer lies in the victim's journey. What did he do? Who did he meet? What questions did he ask? And most importantly, what discoveries did he make?"

"I suggest we put ourselves in his shoes, taking into account his travel objectives, and try to retrace the same route. We know that his first objective was to meet his maternal grandparents, and the next one, according to the information you obtained from his mother, was to find out the exact circumstances of his biological father's death."

"Exactly, my friend Peter, that's what we're going to do," Max continued.

They made a game plan to meet all the people who might have come into contact with James Charles and to visit all the places he could have visited. They agreed to review the plan after the interviews with the inn staff.

At the appointed time, Hercules Simpson welcomed

Maximilien Le Gardeur and Peter Monrose into his office with a broad smile. It was evident that he had been occupying this office for several years, as it was filled with nearly a hundred objects, artifacts, and photographs, resembling a true museum. There was even a large wooden mural that displayed three hatchets with carved handles, including an ivory portion at the end. His solid oak desk remained the centerpiece of the cluttered decor, with a giant fan rotating slowly and smoothly above it.

"*Bonjour*, Monsieur Le Gardeur, and welcome to Sainte-Lucie," he said, immediately inviting them to take a seat in the two armchairs facing his desk.

"Thank you... How should I address you?" Maximilien asked.

"You can call me commandant, that's my official title."

"Liar! Liar!" A voice rang out in the room.

Maximilien hadn't noticed before, but there was a parrot perched on a stand in the corner of the room, all the way in the back. The bird was multicolored, with shades of red, blue, green, and yellow immediately catching the eye.

"Jacquot, be quiet... Please excuse him, that's the only word he knows how to say," said the commandant.

"It's a beautiful animal," remarked Max.

"It's the emblematic bird of Sainte-Lucie, commonly known as Jacquot. It's the chameleon parrot. By moving its feathers, it turns completely green to blend in with the foliage of the trees. I acquired him from an old fisherman who constantly exaggerated the number and size of his catches," the commandant said with a laugh.

Maximilien and his companion sat down on the chairs. The investigator noticed that the commandant's chair, behind the desk, was higher, giving him an air of dominance over his interlocutors.

"Your reputation precedes you, Monsieur Le Gardeur," said Simpson once they were settled. "I asked one of my officers to do some research on you, and I must admit that your background is impressive."

Max only offered a small smile of gratitude.

"I have assigned Officer Monrose to assist you in your investigation. I hope he has been helpful to you so far," the commandant continued, glancing at Peter. "He is at your complete disposal," he added.

"Liar! Liar!" the parrot cried out again.

"Thank you, and I confirm that he has already been a valuable asset," responded Max, briefly turning toward Jacquot. "We have reviewed the various reports regarding the death of the victim in room 11 of the *Golden Apple Inn*, and I must be frank with you, I find the report produced by your office somewhat one-sided and lacking in detail, if I may say so," Maximilien began.

"You think so?" exclaimed the commandant, giving his visitor an inquisitive look.

"Your deductions stop at the initial findings, and you have only recorded two statements. I do not doubt the cause of death, but I question the events that preceded the tragedy, namely the victim's whereabouts on the island during the two weeks leading up to his death. For your information, James Charles came to Sainte-Lucie to, one, meet with members of his maternal family, and two, uncover the truth about the death of his biological father, Charlie Liverpool," Max said, pausing before continuing. "You must remember the incident that occurred twenty years ago on your territory and under your jurisdiction," he concluded, carefully observing the commandant's reaction.

"Monsieur Le Gardeur, firstly, with regards to James Charles, we all lament this tragic and regrettable incident. The investigation that you find simplistic has been corroborated by the chief coroner. As for the victim's movements on the island, you have full latitude to conduct your own investigation, but I consider your work to only serve to answer certain questions from James Charles' mother. Therefore, it will have no legal authority over the case in question." Secondly, yes, I knew the late Charlie Liverpool very well. He was one of the star players in the West Indies cricket team's trio. I was the assistant coach of that team at the time.

"Look at these photos," he said, pointing to the wall on his right. "I appear in them with the famous trio."

"Yes, Charlie's disappearance was a painful moment for his family and all the team members," he concluded with a few tremors in his voice.

"On this one, you are alone with one of the trio members. Who is he?" asked Max.

"Ah, the great Nigel! The leader," replied the commander, regaining his vigor.

Maximilian noticed the pride emanating from his face.

"I must end our meeting now. I have an engagement in the city center, but I am available for a future visit, if necessary."

"It will be necessary. Would next Monday work for you?" asked Max.

"Mondays are impossible. It's my day for deep-sea fishing. I go every Monday, rain or shine. I invite you to check with my office to find out my availability for other days of the week."

With that, the commander stood up, inviting his visitors to leave the office. As they were leaving, Jacquot spoke up again, "Liar! Liar!"

Chapter 03

Later that afternoon at the inn, Max looked at the list he had obtained from JJ.

☐ Amanda Still, housekeeping attendant, eight to two, Monday to Friday.

"Amanda, can I ask you to describe the room as it was in the morning when you found the body lying on the floor?" asked Maximilien, who was in room 11 with Peter and the young woman.

"Well, the first thing I noticed was that the bed had not been slept in and the lights were still on."

"So, the room was intact as if you had completed your daily cleaning," added Peter.

"Yes, I believe… Oh! I remember! There was an unopened KFC lunch box and a bottle of Coca-Cola on the dresser."

Maximilien showed her some pictures taken by the police and asked her to confirm that the victim's body was in the same position as shown in the photos.

"Yes," she replied.

"And his clothing?"

"He was wearing denim pants and a short-sleeved shirt…"

"What kind of shoes was he wearing?"

"Black Nike-style espadrilles."

"Was he wearing socks?" Max asked.

"I couldn't say. His lowered pants covered his legs and part of his shoes."

"So, it was impossible to see the bite wound at first glance," Max asked.

"I didn't notice it," Amanda replied.

"What can you tell me about the victim? Did he talk to you about his stay in Saint Lucia?" Max continued.

"Other than greetings and friendly smiles here and there, no. But I learned the reasons for his trip by talking to Julietta."

Maximilien thanked her and said that would be all for now.

The questioning of the other staff members would take place in the small waiting room of the inn, adjacent to the reception area and rather secluded to preserve the privacy inherent in this kind of conversation.

☐ Oscar Phillip, gardener and handyman, seven to two, Monday to Friday.

Oscar showed up in the small waiting room, as requested. He had kept his work clothes on, except for his rubber boots. Tall, thin, in his sixties, his skin wrinkled by long hours in the sun, he had a slightly dazed look.

"Hello, Mr. Phillip, thank you for agreeing to participate in this interrogation," Max greeted him.

Oscar stared at him as if it had been ten years, if not more, since he had been addressed by his last name. Max invited him to sit down.

"Your gardens are wonderful, and well maintained," Max said, trying to create a warm connection with the gardener.

It had little effect. Peter decided to intervene in Creole.

"We would like to hear from you about the break-in in

room 11," Peter said in Creole.

After listening to Peter speak in the language, Oscar turned to Max.

"It's impossible for the Kravat to have made it to the room on its own. There has never been a venomous snake on this side of the island… The Kravat only lives in banana plantations and other damp areas in the forest. It hides under fallen banana leaves."

"But I saw banana trees in your gardens," Max said, making the connection between the words Kravat and fer de lance.

"I clean the grounds every day. If there were Kravat in my gardens, I would have been bitten a long time ago," Oscar said, almost challenging him.

"So, you're telling me that the fer de lance could have ended up in the room only if someone put it there?" Max intervened.

Oscar did not answer, judging that his words already contained the answer. Peter and Max tried to get additional information, but Oscar fell into a suspicious silence, as if he feared he had said too much. After several attempts, several questions, even in Creole from Peter, Oscar remained silent, as if muzzled by fear. He muttered the following words as he stood up to leave the room:

"The mongoose… The mongoose is dangerous."

Peter and Maximilien made no comment and let him go.

☐ Julietta Clarkson, the housekeeping attendant, from ten a.m. to four p.m. Tuesday to Saturday.

Julietta entered sobbing somewhat. She immediately

expressed her distress and explained how this tragedy had devastated her. Of medium height, with her long black hair braided African style and her friendly face, Julietta projected joy while radiating a certain naivete.

"I'm so sad. We were just getting to know each other... I'm not sure, but I think he had a crush on me... Anyway, I was in love," she said, trying to get comfortable in the chair.

"I see. That's why your testimony will be very important for us so that we can trace his journey on the island since his arrival," Max replied.

"I'm ready," Julietta said.

Julietta mentioned that from the first time their eyes met at the inn, a feeling of affection had easily developed between them. He had confided in her about the reasons for his trip and had needed help to guide him on this journey. His first move was to meet his maternal grandparents. He had the name of his grandmother's hair salon in downtown Castries. His mother had told him that the salon was located between the Basilica of the Immaculate Conception and the Bank of Saint Lucia.

I showed him how to get there. He had to take the 1A Gros-Islet Castries bus from the main road.

***

Seventeen Days Ago, on Monday, April 18

James Charles was finishing his breakfast when Julietta walked through the dining room to see Annetta in the kitchen. He lifted his head to offer her a smile, which made her blush. She smiled back at him. As she walked back, he called out to her, "Good morning, Miss."

"Good morning, Mr. Charles; how are you today?"

"Very well, thank you. I'm going to Castries this morning," he declared.

"Don't forget, from the main road, at the top of the hill, you need to take the A1 Gros-Islet Castries bus and ask the driver to drop you off at the downtown stop."

"Yes, I'll remember, thank you," he replied.

Once outside, James climbed the hill and positioned himself to see the minivan buses pass by. When he saw the A1 number, he signaled for it to stop and got on. Fifteen minutes later, he got off at the downtown stop. Two huge cruise ships were docked in the Castries port, causing a lot of traffic. The presence of one of these huge ships meant that on average, a thousand tourists spent the day going from one shop to another looking for a souvenir of the island.

He was quickly able to identify the basilica, and as his mother had told him, the hair salon was right there, next to the bank. It was a small shop with a window displaying a multitude of braids and wigs. James was excited as he pushed open the front door. Immediately, a woman in her forties came toward him and snobbishly said, "What are you looking for? We only style women's hair here."

"I'm sorry to bother you; I'm looking for Mrs. Charles."

"Mrs. Charles? There is no Mrs. Charles here," she replied.

At the same time, an old lady emerging from the back of the shop walked toward him with a surprised look. She placed the palm of her hand on James's face before sliding it along his cheek and then removing it.

"You're looking for Mrs. Charles? Why? Who are you?" she asked him.

James wasn't sure if he should reveal his identity.

"My name is James Charles, I'm her grandson."

"You look so much like…"

She didn't finish her sentence.

"Mrs. Charles doesn't have a grandson," she corrected herself with a questioning look.

"My mother's name is Jessica Charles."

The old woman smiled widely with surprise and joy. She approached Charles to give him a hug. She then mentioned that she had worked with his grandmother for thirty years, and had known his mother well. This was followed by a long conversation during which she wanted news of Jessica. She told him that his grandmother had sold the business, and now lived in Choiseul, near Vieux Fort.

"How do I get to Choiseul?"

"Are you familiar with the bus system?"

"Yes."

"Then, go back to the downtown terminus and take the B1 Castries Vieux-Fort. Ask the driver for the bus number that goes to Choiseul. Your grandmother lives in a small canary yellow house near the fish market and the church. You can't miss it."

***

"And how did his meeting with his grandparents go?" Peter asked.

"He came back thrilled and fulfilled. His grandmother was so happy to hear news of her daughter after all this time, and to see her grandson, of course. James mentioned that she told him he was a gift from heaven," Julietta replied.

Maximilien asked her to talk about his other outings. She indicated the other places for which he had asked for information and directions, including the Saint Lucia civil registry office. Julietta confided that one day he had returned from the Castries police station with an angry look on his face. This last comment was met with astonishment from Maximilien and Peter, who looked at each other with a suspicious expression.

"I wanted to know more, but he didn't want to talk about it," Julietta added.

"On what day exactly did he go to the police station?" Max asked.

"Let me remember. Um... It was the Thursday after his arrival... The 21st, yes, that's it, April 21."

"Thank you, Julietta, that will be all for now. We'll have to do some research before continuing this interrogation," Max concluded.

"May I go and inform his grandparents in Choiseul? They're probably not aware," Julietta asked.

"Certainly. You seem to be the designated person for this difficult task," Max replied.

She left the small living room and Max turned to Peter to question him about Julietta's last comment. Peter honestly admitted that he was not aware of James' visit to the police station. He remembered being on the road all day on Thursday, April 21.

"Here's what I've gathered so far: It's likely that the fer de lance was deliberately introduced into room 11; Commander Hercule Simpson didn't react to the name Charlie Liverpool, so there's a possibility he was aware of James Charles' quest on the island; and James probably obtained information about his biological father's death that bothered him, or at least didn't satisfy him," Max enumerated.

"If you don't mind, I'll check the investigation archives to identify the file related to Charlie Liverpool's death."

"Definitely, and please check the activity log at the police station for the days of Thursday, April 21, and Monday, May 2," Max added.

The two men took a few seconds to reflect. Many thoughts were racing through Maximilien's head. He was constantly thinking about his conversation with Commander Simpson. Suddenly, the word mongoose came to his mind.

"You didn't react when the gardener mentioned the word mongoose. Is this the first time you've heard it?" Max asked Peter.

"No, but I think it's just an urban legend," Peter replied.

"An urban legend?"

"Yes, we use this word to refer to a character who imposes his authority; who has a hold over individuals, like a vulture hovering over its prey," Peter explained.

"Really?"

☐ Annetta, the cook, worked from seven to ten in the morning and from five to eight in the evening, Monday to Saturday.

Annetta's interrogation was brief. She emphasized the sadness she felt for James and mentioned that one morning he had asked her for advice on tracing his biological father's family, Charlie Liverpool. The name made her jump. Everyone knew Charlie and the tragic event that caused his death twenty years ago.

"At first, I didn't make the connection with his mother, Jessica Charles. It wasn't until after what happened in the last few days and the rumors that were spread that it all came back to me. I remember his mother well now," she said, making an effort to jog her memory.

Max asked, "What memory do you have in mind?"

"She and Josephine had entered the Miss West Indies competition. They were the most beautiful women on the island at the time," she replied, trying to recall the past.

Annetta continued her testimony by mentioning that at the time, there was a great mystery surrounding the mysterious death of Charlie Liverpool and the disappearance of Jessica Charles. She referred to Nigel Glenwood, the owner of the inn, and Charlie's great friend.

☐ Joséphine Jackson, the establishment's manager, worked from seven to four, Monday to Saturday.

Joséphine went to the small sitting room as agreed after refreshing her makeup, which Max immediately noticed. She sat in the chair that was designated for her and offered a radiant smile to the two men.

"How is your investigation going, Mr. Maximilien? What a beautiful name... May I call you by your first name?" she asked.

"Certainly, Joséphine," he replied with a touch of regret.

"I hope the staff is cooperating," she said.

"Excellent cooperation," replied Max. "May I ask under what circumstances you found the position you currently hold?"

"I knew the owner in my youth, Nigel Glenwood. In fact, you'll be meeting him. He'll be here next week."

"So, I deduce that you knew the late Charlie Liverpool," Max said.

"Yes, he left us so young," she replied with a dramatic air.

"And you knew Jessica Charles, the victim's mother," Max continued.

This last question changed the mood in the room. Joséphine took a sudden breath and sat up straight in her chair. Max could imagine the gears turning in her head. She exhaled.

"Monsieur Le Gardeur, yes, I knew Jessica well, but I swear I never made the connection between James Charles and Jessica Charles."

"Even though the victim's name on the inn's registration was James Charles Liverpool?" Max asked.

"Are you insinuating that I have something to do with the death of this young man?" she exclaimed with urgency and defensiveness.

"I'm not insinuating anything, madame. I'm just asking questions," Max replied.

"Well then, the answer is no. No, I didn't make any connection at the time of the registration. It was the chief coroner who informed me later of the victim's mother's name. And that's when rumors started circulating in town."

"One last question, if you don't mind, madame," Max said.

"If it's to accuse me, I can do without it," Joséphine said with aplomb.

"No, don't worry, it's too early for accusations," he replied with a hint of sarcasm. "What kind of relationship did you have with Jessica, Nigel, and Charlie twenty years ago?"

Once again, the question bothered her. Not letting it shake her, she recounted the whole story of the Miss West Indies pageant, her rivalry with Jessica, and the World Cricket Championship. She admitted that she and Jessica were close with some members of the cricket team.

"Thank you, madam, that will be all for now," said Max.

"For your information, Charlie Roy, the assistant manager, and Justin Owen, the driver, had to leave the premises."

"Thank you for letting us know, that works for us. We have enough information to explore new leads. We will question them later, possibly at the end of the week... Oh, by the way, do you know about the mongoose?" he asked as she was about to leave.

"I don't understand. What do you mean?"

"It's okay, thank you," said Max, giving up his last question.

Joséphine left the room with relief. Max turned to Peter.

"So, my friend Peter, what do you make of all this?"

"Are you serious about Madame Josephine's involvement in Charles James's death?" Peter asked.

"I am investigating, considering all possibilities. That being said, I believe she told us the truth."

"So far, all the information we've gathered takes us back twenty years, as if this tragedy, James's death, was related to the Miss West Indies pageant and the World Cricket Championship. That's what I think right now."

"I think so too, my friend. It will be interesting to meet and question Nigel Glenwood," said Max.

"And Madame Jessica Charles," added Peter.

Max suggested ending the day by going to the morgue. After all, neither of them had seen the victim. Peter recommended taking a water taxi from the inn's dock to downtown to avoid afternoon traffic. The taxi was called and they set off for the sea.

After leaving the inhabited area of Marisule, they took the short, unpaved path leading to the shore. The hot and humid

Caribbean temperature had reached its peak for the day. The few black flies at this time of day made the heat more unbearable, and Max removed his linen jacket.

Along the way, they passed what appeared to be an old, large chicken coop. Vegetation had long since overtaken it. Max noticed a few small trees adorned with green fruits oversized compared to the tree and its skeletal branches.

"It looks like big green Christmas balls hanging on a scrawny tree," Max said, wiping his forehead.

"It's the calabash tree, the iconic tropical tree of Saint Lucia. The fruit is used to make containers, large bowls," replied Peter.

The water taxi was waiting for them. The trip was short, barely ten minutes. The boat made its way between two cruise ships and docked at the public pier. Maximilien was surprised by the proximity of the huge cruise ships moored there.

"Does that surprise you?" The shuttle captain threw at him. "The port of Castries is the deepest of all the others in the various tourist destinations in the Caribbean."

"It's definitely an advantage," Max replied.

"It was also an advantage in times of war," the captain retorted.

An auto-patrol was waiting for them, and the journey to the morgue was quick. It was located in the heights of Castries, and its facade reflected its vocation, gray, dull, and windowless. The morgue attendant led them to the medico-legal laboratory. The coffin-drawer was already open, and the sheet lifted. The two men approached to examine the body. Despite the bluish color of the skin, the youth of the victim still emerged. All of this made James Charles' accidental death all the more sad and heartbreaking.

"Too bad the bite caused the violent contact with the hook,

because the anti-poison emergency team could have saved him," a man wearing a white coat said as he approached the two men.

He was standing back in the room, and Max had not noticed him before.

"Hello, my name is Samuel Davies. I'm the medical examiner," he said.

"Hello. Maximilien Le Gardeur, and this is my colleague, Peter Monrose, whom you probably know," Max replied.

Samuel Davies nodded. According to him, if the victim had been able to manifest the fact that he had been bitten by a snake to the people present at the inn, the staff would have contacted the anti-poison emergency team.

"An anti-poison injected no later than four to six hours after the bite could have made a difference," the medical examiner said.

They discussed some of the technical analysis he had performed. Max wanted to make sure that a sample had been taken for potential DNA tests, which the medical examiner confirmed. However, he explained that for deoxyribonucleic acid analyses, he had to deal with the laboratory in Martinique or Cuba. This could take a week, including transfer, analysis, and results.

Max and Peter made their way back to the embarkation dock for the return to the inn. The day was drawing to a close. It had been decided that at dawn, they would head for Choiseul. Before leaving Max, Peter mentioned that on the way back, he would stop at the police station to request the Liverpool file and learn about the activities at the station for Thursday, April 21, and Monday, May 2.

***

It was almost six in the evening and the sun had just drawn the curtain for the night. Max decided to pass through the dining room. Annetta was there. He ordered a gin and tonic to take to his room. *A good cigar before dinner would be well-deserved*, he thought to himself, taking his first sip and walking toward his room. Upon his arrival, he grabbed his cell phone and saw that he had received a text message and a phone call.

The text message was from Jessica Charles, informing him that she had landed in Saint Lucia and would be staying at Bel Jou, a mountain-side resort in Castries. He pressed the phone icon. His hands trembled with excitement. The call was from his daughter, France Cardinal.

The last time they had seen each other was at Eric's funeral. France had disowned her father after her brother's death, accusing him of being the cause. She reproached him for pressuring Eric to enroll in the Kingston Military College to become a fighter pilot and follow in his footsteps, contrary to Eric's aspirations, which were geared toward artistic creativity.

Eric had often confided in France to convey his pain and inability to confess to their father his indifference to military life. He preferred to leave the family nest and wander from one friend's family to another before joining a street gang. His drug consumption had increased, as well as his involvement in drug trafficking.

France had even changed her last name to take her mother's, Cardinal. This gesture, made shortly after the funeral, devastated Maximilien. The divorce from his wife followed a few years later. It had been twelve years since France and Maximilien had spoken. The only news he received about his daughter came from his ex-wife.

Max tried to call her back, but each attempt ended with the

same message: "Your call cannot be completed as dialed." He tried to send her a text message, but each time the system indicated: "Undelivered."

He abandoned trying for the time being. He opened his cigar box, chose one, and went to sit on his patio. Once he had lit it, he began to reflect on this difficult period in his life. Yes, now he was aware of his mistakes. He had done everything to appease his daughter's anger following the death of his son; he had apologized, acknowledged his wrongs, and begged her to forgive him. Nothing had worked.

But why had she tried to reach him after all these years? He wondered.

Furthermore, he was out of the country and unavailable. He wiped away some tears that were making their way to his mouth.

He took his cell phone to respond to Jessica's text message.

Chapter 04

Saturday, May 7, 2005

From Castries, there were two routes to get to Choiseul: the main road that crossed the island, or the secondary road that connected all the fishing villages on the Caribbean coast. Peter and Max had opted for the secondary road, which meant zigzagging up and down between each village.

The climbs up to the steep and dizzying cliffs overlooking the Caribbean Sea were exhilarating and thrilling. Each summit offered panoramic views of the sea and the few cottages perched on the cliffside.

"Off in the distance, you can see Saint Vincent and the Grenadines," Peter said to Max while staying focused on the road.

The descents required more rigorous driving until they arrived in the villages nestled in the alcoves. The villages passed by: Marigot Bay, Anse la Raye, Canaries, Soufriere, Choiseul, and further away, Laborie.

They had left early that morning. Max wanted to meet Jessica's parents before her arrival. The night before, they had exchanged several text messages. Jessica had mentioned that she had to go to the morgue in the morning for the identification protocol, and then to the presbytery of the Basilica of Saint Lucia to organize the funeral.

It was Max who told her about her parent's move to

Choiseul after the sale of the hair salon. He gave her instructions on how to find their home. Jessica had asked him to tell them that she couldn't wait to see them and that she would visit them as soon as she finished the administrative procedures in Castries.

"Here we are," Peter said, making a turn to take the road leading to the center of the village.

"There's the church," Max said as they passed by the open-air fish market at the port.

The wooden church, painted in a powder blue, except for the white frames of the windows and doors, dominated the whole village. The yellow house was quickly identified. Peter parked the car. It was nine-thirty, and the streets were almost deserted. In these small coastal villages, the inhabitants worked at the port until about nine o'clock, and then resumed their activities at the fish market when the fishermen returned around midday. The fish found buyers quickly.

Although fishing was the main survival occupation, Choiseul was known for its cultural and artistic activities. In fact, most of the craft products sold in the kiosks in Castries were made here, such as the famous bowls made from the fruit of the calabash tree.

Max noticed an old man trying unsuccessfully to reach a mango. The tree took up the entire small plot in front of the house and provided shade for its gallery. Dressed plainly, the man wore overalls with a white undershirt.

"May I?" Max interjected.

The man looked at him and stepped back a few feet, glancing over at Peter who was wearing a blouse adorned with his captain's insignia.

"Ah, there it is," Max said, handing him the fruit.

"Thanks, stranger. If you can give me that one too, I'll invite you to taste it," the man challenged.

Max complied, and Peter stepped forward to introduce themselves and explain the reason for their visit. Julietta had come to see them the night before, and Max expressed his sympathies.

"Come, I'll go get my wife," he said, inviting them to take a seat on the veranda. "As you can imagine, she's much shaken," he said before opening the screened door.

The elderly woman appeared on the threshold a few moments later. Wearing a white shirt dress and a Jacquot the parrot-themed apron, she had her hair tied up with a multicolored scarf. The gray-haired woman looked at the two men and decided to push the door open. They stood up to greet her and offer their condolences. Her face betrayed several hours of tears as she expressed her grief.

"The young woman, Julietta, informed me of your presence on the island. You spoke to Jessica. Has she arrived?" Mrs. Charles asked.

"Yes, ma'am, she arrived yesterday evening," Max replied. "She asked me to let you know that she needed to take care of some administrative tasks in Castries this morning, but she'll come see you as soon as everything is settled. She's very excited to see both of you again."

The elderly woman sighed with melancholy joy.

"What a sad irony! I discover and lose a grandson whose existence I didn't even know, and I'll find my daughter whom I thought I'd never see again," she said with a mixture of bitterness, sadness, and bliss.

"Mrs. Charles, without wanting to bother you too much in these difficult times, I would like to talk to you about James,"

Max said.

"Is it true that his biological father is Charlie Liverpool?" she asked, ignoring his last comment.

"According to your daughter, yes," Max replied.

"Hmm..."

"James came to visit you on Monday, April 18, according to what Julietta told us. Is that true?" Max inquired.

"Yes, it was a—indescribable shock. He was there trying to convince me that he was Jessica Charles's son. I was crying and telling him it was impossible. I couldn't believe it, but at the same time, I was filled with joy."

Meanwhile, Mr. Charles arrived with a tray of mango and melon pieces. They all took a moment to taste the fruit before Maximilien resumed the conversation. He asked them to share the conversations they had with their grandson. Mr. Charles mentioned that James had visited them twice, on Monday, the 18th, and the following Monday, the 25th. He then continued to answer Max's request.

The first time, after the festivities of their reunion, the conversations centered around the last twenty years: Jessica's life in London, James' studies. He asked us several questions about our life in Saint Lucia over the past sixty-five years: whether he had uncles, aunts, cousins, who his great-grandparents were... all in good spirits. But I remember the second time he arrived a bit annoyed.

"Yes," the old woman interrupted. "He still hadn't been able to find his biological father's family, and he was expressing some frustration about his search for information on his death."

"What kind of frustration?" Max asked.

"He complained about the lack of cooperation from the authorities," she replied. "From what he told me, he had a lot of difficulty getting information about his father's accident."

"Yes, and when he finally gained access to the investigation file, he found little information: a few typewritten and yellowed forms, an old article from the local newspaper with the headline 'Accidental death of cricket champion Charlie Liverpool,'" added Mr. Charles.

"Did he tell you about his next steps?" Peter asked.

"He said he absolutely had to talk to his paternal grandparents to learn more," Mr. Charles replied.

The elderly couple had known Charlie Liverpool as a member of the famous fer de lance trio, but had no information to help James locate his paternal grandparents.

Maximilien thanked them for the interview and wished them good luck with their reunion with their daughter. The two men took the main island road back this time, avoiding the narrow and winding roads of the Caribbean coast, even if it meant taking a detour through Vieux Fort.

"I wanted to mention this to you this morning, I couldn't get hold of the investigation file. The archives office closes earlier on Fridays. I'll go as soon as they open on Monday," said Peter.

"Yes, I'm looking forward to reading the article about Charlie Liverpool's so-called accidental death," replied Max. "Do whatever you can to get the file earlier."

"I understand, I'll see what I can do," Peter agreed.

"We absolutely must locate Charlie's parents. I'm counting on you for this task," said Max.

"Okay. I hope they're still alive," Peter replied, briefly looking away from the road to face Max.

During the journey, Maximilien took the opportunity to ask Peter about his family, his studies, and his entry into the

Castries police force. He wanted to learn more about his work at the station and the leadership of the commander.

***

Jessica was supposed to meet the chief coroner, Albert Monfils, at the morgue at ten o'clock. He was waiting outside, looking sharp as ever. When she arrived, he introduced himself and offered his condolences.

"Are you ready to perform this procedure, Mrs. Charles?" Albert asked her, his voice laced with respect.

"Yes, thank you," Jessica replied.

He invited her inside, where Commander Hercule Simpson and the medical examiner, Samuel Davies, were waiting in the forensic laboratory. Jessica and Hercule locked eyes for a few seconds. After the customary introductions and expressions of condolences, the doctor pulled out the coffin drawer and, after glancing at Jessica for her consent, lifted the sheet.

She took a step forward and, remaining strong, placed her hand on James's forehead and ran it through his hair. A thought came to her mind: "I escaped from the island with a son, and twenty years later, the island takes him back from me..."

Jessica kissed James's forehead and let her tears flow freely. Albert kindly supported her. She simply said to him, "It's my son James, James Charles!"

She turned around to leave the room, and the others followed. Outside, Hercule approached her.

"I'm sorry, Jessica, for the accident that caused your son's death," he said, confirming that he remembered her.

She looked at him without saying a word and, turning to Albert Monfils, asked him, "Can you drop me off at the Basilica of the Immaculate Conception?"

"Certainly, please follow me. My car is parked right next to us," he replied, glancing at the two men and signifying the end of the administrative exercise.

***

Peter dropped Max off at the inn and left immediately. It was three o'clock. Maximilien spotted Julietta sitting in the shade on a bench at the entrance to the garden of large fruit trees. He headed toward her.

"Good morning, Mr. Le Gardeur," she greeted him with a natural smile.

"Please, stay seated," Max said as she got up. "May I?" he added, indicating the bench.

"Of course," she replied, sliding over to make room for him. "I'm waiting for my cousin to come and pick me up to take me home."

"I wanted to thank you for your visit to James's grandparents. It shows a lot of empathy on your part," Max said.

"You know, it was so nice to meet his grandparents, despite everything," she said.

"I would like to go back to your comments about James's visit to the police station. I know he remained discreet after that, but please, make an effort and try to remember if, in the following days, he had any comments about his quest for the truth about his biological father's death," he asked her cordially.

Julietta took a few seconds to think out loud, trying to remember her conversations with James. She ended up confessing that James would express things like, "One day he told me this…" And "another time he expressed anger about…"

"Is this the kind of information you were looking for?" she asked candidly.

"They are relevant to my investigation, thank you," he replied.

"Ah! There's my cousin, goodbye, Monsieur Le Gardeur," she said as she stood up.

"One last question, if you don't mind… In all your exchanges with James, did he mention the name of the police station commander, Hercule Simpson?"

"From memory, no," Julietta answered cautiously. "I must go now."

"All right. Thank you."

In turn, Maximilien stood up and headed toward his room. He chose to go through the garden of small blooming shrubs. As soon as the patio door of his room was opened, he searched for his cellphone. He had forgotten it again when he left early this morning for Choiseul. No calls had come in, but he had a text message waiting for him.

It was from Jessica, who informed him that the funeral would take place on Monday, May 9, at the Basilica of the Immaculate Conception in Castries at ten o'clock. She added that she would be free the next day to meet him according to his availability. She left her number.

Later that evening, he received a message from Peter, who said, "Good news, I got my hands on the Charlie Liverpool file. I'll bring it to you tomorrow after the religious services and Sunday brunch. Hoping that works for you."

***

Sunday, May 8, 2005

Maximilien got up and, after freshening up, went to the reception. Charlie Roy, the assistant manager, was on duty. Max explained his difficulty in reaching a family member in Canada by phone. Charlie offered him to use the inn's line.

"We have a private phone booth in the small lounge. I'll give you access to the line. Dial the international access code 011, then the country code 1 for Canada, and finally, the local number of your family member."

"Thank you."

Max entered the cramped room, picked up the receiver, and as soon as he heard the tone, dialed the numbers as instructed. He had to wait fifteen seconds before hearing a ring. A few seconds later, a voice came through the receiver: "Hello, you've reached France Cardinal. I can't take your call right now. Please leave me a message, and I'll call you back as soon as possible."

"Hello... France, it's your father! I missed your call, I apologize. Please call me back... I'm currently out of the country. Bye... I hope everything is okay," he ended, touched.

After hanging up, he sat on the small stool in the phone booth for a few minutes, looking dejected.

In the dining room, Max was surprised not to see Annetta but rather a man in his fifties, who greeted him. Short in stature, dressed in black pants and a white shirt with a bow tie, the man did not look like a kitchen employee.

Max remembered it was Sunday.

"Good morning, Monsieur Le Gardeur!" greeted Justin Owen, the chauffeur and assistant cook of the inn.

"Good day to you, I see; it's Annetta's day off," replied Maximilien, introducing himself to Justin.

"Pleasure to meet you! Annetta told me what you like for breakfast. I'll bring it to you in a moment. Please, take a seat," Justin said, gesturing to a chair.

"Starting with a coffee would be appreciated, thank you," Max requested as he sat down.

He wanted to talk to Annetta and had some questions for her. He remembered that she lived in the Marisule neighborhood and decided to visit her after breakfast.

Soon Justin placed Max's breakfast in front of him. Without prompting, Justin began speaking about the tragedy that had occurred at the inn the week before, the death of James Charles.

"Such a tragic story," Max remarked.

Justin then told Max about his conversations with James and how James had once asked him to drive him somewhere.

"He wanted to go to the civil registry of Saint Lucia. He wanted to check birth, marriage, and death records," Justin recounted.

"Did he mention the names of the people involved in those records?" Max asked.

"No," Justin replied.

"Thank you for the information. Tell me, do you know where Annetta's house is?" Max inquired.

"Yes, you go up the hill toward the main road. You'll see a small alley on the right. The first house is the Glenwood's, and the third is Annetta's," Justin answered.

"Glenwood, isn't that the family name of the owner of the *Golden Apple*?" Max inquired further.

"Yes and the house at the top of the hill is where his parents live. The father has passed away, but Mrs. Glenwood still lives there with her oldest son," Justin informed.

Max thanked Justin again and went to his room to grab his kaki Tilley hat for the walk he was about to take. The sun was already beating down hard on his head and neck.

The Marisule neighborhood had about forty properties, all different from one another: some large, some small, some with immaculate landscaping, others left to the mercy of Mother Nature. When Max reached the alley, he was surprised to see that the Glenwood residence looked more like a farmhouse than an estate. A crudely built chicken coop, dying banana trees, renovated doghouses, and a small pigsty took up the entire front of the house. Due to the overgrown vegetation, it was even difficult to discern the dwelling.

Max spotted a man dressed like a gardener who was working near the chicken coop. Before Max could even greet him, an enormous pit-bull mastiff emerged from one of the doghouses and charged toward him, fury in its eyes. After running about fifteen feet, a chain caused the dog to perform an acrobatic flip. Despite this, it landed on its feet and, barking loudly and drooling, kept its gaze fixed on the intruder.

"Rex... Rex... Calm down, back," the gardener ordered, continuing his activities and ignoring the visitor.

"Excuse me, is this the Glenwood house?" Max asked after recovering from his scare.

"You're sharp, right on the money," the man replied sarcastically.

"I introduce myself..." Max began.

"I know who you are," the man cut him off.

"Are you Nigel Glenwood's older brother, the owner of the inn?" Max inquired.

"My half-brother. Nigel, the great Nigel, is my half-brother," the man grumbled.

"And what's your name?" asked Max, ignoring his last statement.

Clinton Glenwood introduced himself. Despite his unpleasant attitude, Maximilien eventually won him over when Clinton learned that Max was a former fighter pilot. The jets, their speed, and aerial acrobatics fascinated him. From that moment on, Clinton opened up and gave Maximilien a history lesson.

Clinton told him that his father, Archibald Glenwood, had died of a heart attack two years earlier. The plot of land where Marisule now stood had belonged to Archibald and his grandparents, who ran a chicken farm on the flat part of the land near the shores of the Caribbean Sea. Twenty years earlier, they had officially surveyed the land to subdivide it and sell the lots to individuals. That was how Marisule had developed. At twenty, his father had confided in him that Nigel was not his brother, but his half-brother, and ordered him not to reveal this information to avoid damaging his celebrity status. Under pressure from his wife, Archibald had conceded a piece of land to Nigel, where the *Golden Apple Inn* now stood. In his will, he had fairly bequeathed all his belongings to his wife and his son Clinton, who lived with his mother in the family home. He had never married.

"This is the first time I've told anyone that my brother is actually my half-brother. Please, for the love of my mother, keep this to yourself," Clinton begged, concluding his story.

"I promise," replied Max.

The two men parted ways. It was past noon. Max decided to return to the inn to wait for Peter's arrival. He would see Annetta tomorrow. When Peter showed up, Maximilien invited him to the dining room. Although the inn didn't offer lunch,

Justin still offered them an iced tea, which they accepted.

"Here's the file," Peter said, spreading its contents on the table.

The old, difficult-to-read typewritten forms were there, including the investigation report, Charlie Liverpool's birth and death certificates, samples in a bag that appeared to be pieces of the victim's nails, and a newspaper article from the time.

Accidental Death of Cricket Champion Charlie Liverpool

The famous member of the fer de lance trio, Charlie Liverpool, who had been missing for three days, was found floating in Castries Bay, not far from the promontory of the secret cove. The ongoing investigation led by Chief Investigator Hercule Simpson, rules out suicide and rather considers the possibility of an unfortunate accident.

The body found had multiple fractures and bruises, suggesting a fall from a cliff onto the reef at low tide.

The three members of the West Indies cricket champion team, Nigel Glenwood, Danny Ford, and Charlie Liverpool, had returned to Saint Lucia last Friday to continue the celebrations following their remarkable victory over the British. Excessive revelry may have played a role in this tragic event.

The investigation continues.

"What a terrible death," Max said, placing the document on the table. "Have you noticed that the investigation report suggests suicide or accident, but ignores the possibility of murder?"

"I'd like to know what elements of the investigation led the authorities to dismiss this hypothesis," Peter replied.

"Indeed, my friend, only Commander Simpson can enlighten us. The importance of locating and questioning Charlie Liverpool's parents becomes essential for our own investigation," Maximilien concluded.

Taking the sample bag, Maximilien added, "Unfortunately, the nails are no longer usable for DNA testing. Such samples need to be taken within the first year after death."

Maximilien informed Peter that the funeral service would take place the next day at the Basilica of the Immaculate Conception. They agreed to attend, and Peter assured Max he would pick him up at nine thirty.

***

Monday, May 9, 2005

Around nine fifteen, Maximilien arrived at the reception desk, expecting to find Josephine, but Amanda was there instead.

"JJ is absent because of the funeral," Amanda immediately told him.

"I'm also attending. Have a good day, miss."

"Good day, Mr. Le Gardeur."

Max and Peter arrived in downtown Castries at nine forty-five. Peter found shaded parking along Derek Walcott Park on Laborie Street, adjacent to the basilica.

The Basilica of the Immaculate Conception was built in 1894 under the direction of Brother Scoles, a priest from Demerara. Mostly made of wood, it required constant monitoring to prevent fire. Despite the notice of the religious service published only the day before, there was a crowd.

As soon as Maximilien entered the building, he was struck

by the musty smell of incense and the scent of smoky wood, a product of the tropical heat that had penetrated through the ages, along with the ancient Christian artifacts and interior architecture, giving him the impression of traveling through time.

The open casket was placed at the center of the aisle, toward the front of the church. Jessica Charles and her parents stood halfway between the casket and the entrance, receiving condolences from people. The pace was slow to allow everyone to spend a few minutes paying their respects in front of the casket. Albert Monfils was there, as well as Hercule Simpson, accompanied by a woman.

Maximilien spotted Josephine and went over to greet her. Like all the women present, she wore brightly colored, traditional Antillean clothing for the occasion.

"Hello, Josephine," he said.

"Hello, Mr. Le Gardeur," JJ replied, still remembering their last conversation.

"May I ask who the woman is accompanying Commander Simpson?"

She nodded her head to identify the person in question. "That's Nigel's mother, Mrs. Glenwood. Excuse me, I have to go say hello to someone," she said quickly, trying to slip away.

Max joined the line behind Hercule and Mrs. Glenwood. Jessica noticed him at that moment and, leaning toward her mother, asked if it was indeed Maximilien Le Gardeur. Her mother confirmed it, and Jessica smiled at him from afar to thank him for his presence.

Hercule and Mrs. Glenwood approached Jessica and her parents to offer their condolences. Max, who could hear the exchanges, realized that Mrs. Glenwood and Mrs. Charles' mother knew each other well.

In turn, he greeted Jessica as Hercule and Mrs. Glenwood made their way to the casket to pay their respects.

"Hello, Jessica," he said, glancing toward her parents as a greeting.

"Hello, Mr. Le Gardeur. Thank you for coming," she replied.

"My sympathies…"

As Maximilien was about to continue, a woman's scream was heard, and a small group gathered around the casket. Mrs. Glenwood had cried out and fainted at the sight of the deceased. Hercule had just managed to catch her before she collapsed to the ground. A chair was brought for her to regain her composure. When she came to, she apologized for her weakness. Hercule decided it was best that he escort her back while apologizing on his behalf to Jessica and her parents.

The murmurs of the attendees eventually died down, and the service resumed. The tribute from the deceased's grandmother was particularly moving. She referred to the loss of her unknown grandson and the reunion with her daughter. After the service, the procession departed for the Vigie cemetery, located about ten minutes by car from the basilica. It ran alongside the long Vigie beach, so the guests, dressed in their Sunday best, appreciated the cool breeze blowing in from the sea.

Maximilien spotted Hercule parking his car along the beach under a walnut tree. He assumed that he had decided to return for the remainder of the service after dropping off Mrs. Glenwood. He decided to go and meet him.

Max smiled at the commandant as they met at the funeral. "It's nice of you to come back for the funeral," Max said.

"I thought it was the respectful thing to do," replied the commandant.

"Especially on a Monday, your sacred day for deep-sea fishing," Max teased.

"Sometimes a citizen's duty takes precedence over personal activities," the commandant responded.

"Like on Monday, May 2, the day the tragedy at the *Golden Apple Inn* was discovered," Max added.

"What does that statement mean?" Hercule asked, taken aback.

"It means what it means," Max replied.

As he fixed his gaze on Maximilien, Hercule took a deep breath before speaking with confidence. "I believe we should join the service. I'll wait for you at my office this afternoon at three o'clock," he said before heading back to the ceremony.

***

At three o'clock sharp, Maximilien and Peter arrived at the police station. Max mentioned to Peter that it was better for him to meet the commander alone. Peter nodded, expressing his disappointment with a sigh. The officer at the reception led Maximilien to the commander's office.

"The commander will be with you shortly. Can I offer you a drink?" the officer asked.

"I'd appreciate some tea," Max replied.

"Cold or hot?" the officer asked.

"Iced tea would be wonderful," Max said.

The officer left the room. While waiting for the commander, Maximilien strolled around the office, examining all the objects in it. He waved at Jacquot the parrot, who ignored him and sidestepped on his perch.

"Bravo, bravo, Mr. Investigator, for your comment this morning about Monday fishing," Hercule teased, entering the office. "Please, have a seat."

"Thank you," Maximilien replied, unfazed.

"That Monday you referred to, I had a medical appointment early in the afternoon that I couldn't cancel, so I decided to cancel my fishing trip and come back to the office that morning," Hercule explained.

"I'd like to talk to you about your investigation into Charlie Liverpool's accidental death twenty years ago," Max said, ignoring Hercule's last statement.

"You surprise me, Mr. Le Gardeur. Did you receive a new mandate?" Hercule asked jokingly.

"Liar! Liar!" the parrot screamed.

Maximilien explained to Hercule the facts that led him to believe that the two events, those of young James and his biological father, Charlie Liverpool, were potentially related, or at least that Charlie's death deserved to be re-analyzed. Max knew that these statements were disturbing the commander. He even raised the possibility that both events were not accidental.

Hercule was trying to remain calm, but his discomfort was strongly manifested through his body language, which Maximilien easily detected. Hercule, trying to reverse the power dynamic, stood up and sat on the corner of his desk, in a position that was likely to make him look more imposing to his interlocutor.

"Can I trust you with a secret?" he began.

Maximilien did not answer but signaled that he was ready to listen. Simpson began his argument.

"You are not unaware of the fact that I had a close

relationship with Charlie. He was a great cricket player, but also a great sensitive man. At the time, everything led me to believe that Charlie was experiencing immense heartache. We had just won the World Cricket Championship, and celebrations lasted for a few days after our return to the island. The mix of alcohol, festivities, and heartache would have pushed him to do something desperate... I wanted to protect his parents, who were devout Christians, so I conducted the investigation in a way that concluded with a sad accident. That's the truth," he said, satisfied with himself, before returning to his desk.

Max looked at him for a few seconds, and then stood up. He was about to leave the room, but turned back to the commander.

"Did you meet James Charles during the two weeks prior to his death?"

"Absolutely not, what are you implying?"

"And do you know the mongoose?"

Not letting the commander answer, preferring to let him ponder, Max left the room, but not without greeting Jacquot on the way out.

Chapter 05

Tuesday, May 10, 2005

I absolutely need to have an interview with Jessica today, Maximilien thought as he woke up. He hadn't been able to talk to her since she arrived. At the funeral, she had told him that she was going to spend the night in Choiseul, at her parent's house. He was looking for his cell phone to send her a text message.

Ah! Here it is. "Good morning, Jessica. What time do you plan to be back in Castries? I would like to have a first interview with you. Maximilien. Thank you," he said out loud as he typed his message.

He sent it. As soon as he heard the confirmation sound of the electronic sending, he received a call from Peter. He slid the bar allowing him to accept the communication.

"Hello, Peter!"

"Good morning, Mr. Le Gardeur!"

"I think it's time for you to call me Maximilien or Max."

"Okay, Maximilien! I have good news."

Peter announced that he had located the Liverpools. According to what he had found out, they lived in the small village of Micoud, on the Atlantic side, not far from Vieux Fort. He had not been able to identify the address, but he reassured Max that everyone knew each other in these small fishing villages. The meeting at the inn was scheduled for nine thirty; the village was an hour from Castries.

After breakfast, around nine o'clock, Maximilien went to the reception. JJ was absent for a second day. It was her assistant, Charlie, who was in her place. He confirmed that Josephine had requested another day off following yesterday's funeral.

It was difficult to tell how old Charlie Roy was with his goatee and small round glasses. He was tall, slim; Max guessed he was between thirty and forty. He showed a lot of nervousness in his nonverbal language.

"Were you on duty on the night of the room 11 incident?" Max asked him.

"Yes, why?" he replied, almost frozen with anxiety and straightening his shoulders as if he had been caught red-handed.

"Please don't worry, I just wanted to ask you a few questions," Max said calmly.

"Yes, sure, go ahead."

"Tell me everything you remember about that evening, let's say from five o'clock until you left. I presume you were constantly at the reception?"

"Not all the time. It was a Sunday," Charlie began before continuing his explanation.

He mentioned that he had few guests that evening. Since it was Sunday, the kitchen was closed. He remembered that the guest in room 11 had told him, when he passed by the reception, that he was going to get himself some dinner at KFC.

"What time was it?" asked Maximilien.

"It was half past six," quickly replied Charlie.

He went on to say that it was the last time he had seen him, implying that he must have gone straight back to his room through his patio. He insisted several times that he had not heard anything suspicious that evening. Maximilien let him talk while analyzing his body language.

"Only one couple left that night and came back around eight-thirty," Charlie said.

"And that couple left the day after the victim was discovered," added Max, as it was one of the first things he had asked about upon arrival.

"That's right."

"Thank you. I was told the innkeeper is supposed to arrive from England soon," said Max.

"Yes, tomorrow evening," he replied. "Mr. Simpson will be happy to see him," he added with a hint of excitement in his voice.

"Simpson, the police chief?"

"Yes."

"Why?"

"Well… uh… they're great friends… They won the World Cup of cricket together."

"May I ask your age, if it's not too personal?"

"Forty, soon to be forty-one."

Noting the time, Maximilien thanked him again and left to wait for Peter in the inn's parking area. Peter arrived a few minutes after nine-thirty. They immediately set off for Micoud.

"Don't tell me we have to take the road through the small villages," Max asked as the car took the main road.

"Fear not, the cross-island road, from Castries, passes through the village of Micoud."

Maximilien shared with Peter his impressions following his conversation with Charlie Roy, informing him of his strange behavior when questioned about the night of the tragedy at the inn. Max expressed doubts about the sincerity of his comments. What surprised him was that Charlie had answered quickly and without hesitation about the exact time of James Charles' departure from the inn on the evening before the victim was discovered.

"I'll have to question him again," he concluded.

Along the way, Peter turned into a tourist guide for Max again. He pointed out that the Atlantic waves crashing against the cliffs were more dramatic on this side of the island. They hit the steep cliffs with force, and their surges were striking. Peter told Max that they would soon pass through the village of Dennery, known for its viewpoint located at the village's exit. It offered a captivating panorama of the village, its fishing port, and its protective cliffs against which the waves broke.

"We're here. A few minutes' stop is in order," said Peter.

Maximilien was not disappointed. He took out his phone to take a wide-angle photo of the panorama. A thought came to his mind. He would have liked to send this photo to his daughter, accompanied by a kind word, but he knew she would not appreciate this kind of gesture of reconciliation.

"Maximilien, are you okay?" asked Peter. "You seem lost in your thoughts."

"No, no, I'm fine," he replied, heading toward the car.

A few minutes later, as they were driving, Peter brought up the subject again.

"You know, Maximilien, I can also detect people's emotions, and earlier, on the cliff, you seemed nostalgic… Do you want to talk about it?"

Maximilien hesitated, weighing the relevance of confiding in Peter. He thought of his psychologist, whom he had consulted after the break-up with his daughter. "The best remedy is conversation, sharing one's emotions," the psychologist had told him. He decided to tell Peter about the dramatic event concerning his son, as well as, the abandonment and denial by his daughter. It made him feel better, and Peter proved to be very empathetic in his words. Maximilien thanked him with an appreciative look.

They finally arrived in Micoud. Peter suggested they head to the port. He parked the car right in front of the open-air stone counter of the fishermen, which served to parcel and sell the fruit of their day's work. A wooden gazebo-style roof provided protection from the sun's rays. The place was deserted. Maximilien spotted a man coming out of the small adjacent chapel, examining the hinges of the door. *Possibly a beadle*, he thought. He walked toward him after signaling to Peter to start the conversation.

"Hello, my dear sir," said Peter, displaying his captain's insignia.

"Hello," he replied, casting an inquisitive glance toward Maximilien.

"We're looking for the Liverpool's. According to my research, they've been living in Micoud for about fifteen years. Do you know them?" Peter inquired.

"Is he a journalist?" he retorted, pointing at Max.

"No, we're conducting an investigation. Please, can you tell us where they live?" Peter asked in a more authoritative tone.

The man agreed to their request and informed them of the way to their house. They lived in a small residence half a kilometer from the chapel. A non-drivable uphill alley had to be taken to reach it. Following the caretaker's advice, they left their car where it was parked and began the walk to the Liverpool's house.

After a few minutes, no more than five, they recognized the house as described by the caretaker. Perched on a small promontory, it offered a partial but reasonable view of Choiseul Bay. A man and a woman were working in a small garden at the back of the house. The man, tall and wearing overalls and rubber boots, stood up as the strangers approached and came toward them, while the woman continued to pull out weeds.

"How can I help you?" he asked, noticing Peter's insignia.

"Mr. Liverpool?" said Peter.

"Yes," he replied, as the woman approached the group.

"I am Captain Monrose, and this is Mr. Le Gardeur. We would like to have a conversation with you."

Casting a glance at his wife, he gestured for them to follow him. She too was tall, wearing a gray and navy-blue sports ensemble. There was a small octagonal wooden gazebo on the front corner of the property. It was toward this outdoor shelter that he led them while the woman slipped inside the house.

"We have heard of the sad event that occurred at the *Golden Apple Inn*," he said to them immediately. "I also know that our son's name was mentioned by the gossips in relation to this death. The rumor that Charlie is the biological father of the victim seems impossible to us."

"Why is that?" asked Max, who had remained silent until then.

"It does not reflect the education and values we passed on to him. Charlie was a sensitive person, and he had principles. He would never have, excuse the expression, impregnated a woman before marriage."

"I respect all of that, but the victim's mother told her son that he was his biological father. Did you know Jessica Charles?"

"I knew her mother well," replied Mrs. Liverpool, who arrived in the meantime with a tray which she placed on the central table. "Would you like some iced tea?"

They gladly accepted, given the Caribbean heat which had reached its peak on this day. The breeze coming from the sea was refreshing, but the iced tea was welcome.

"Madame Charles was my hairdresser, but I never mentioned my son during my visits to her salon. I remember her daughter Jessica, but I never heard Charlie mention her name in my presence."

"Neither did I," added Mr. Liverpool.

Maximilien then explained the purpose of his presence on the island: he had been hired by the victim's mother to verify the exact causes of her son's death. He explained to them the reasons for James' stay at Saint Lucia, the victim of the *Golden Apple Inn*. Trying to find out details about the accidental death of his biological father could have been poorly received, he confided. He asked if he could discuss with them the period of their son Charlie's death.

The Liverpool's had left Castries a few years after their son's death, precisely because they could no longer bear discussing this painful event with the community and the local and international media. Several reports had been produced in Saint Lucia and broadcast by sports networks internationally because of the fame of Charlie Liverpool, a member of the famous fer de Lance trio within the West Indies team. Mr. Liverpool looked at his wife, seeking her consent before proceeding with this journey back in time. She gave him a nod. Maximilien captured this agreement and dove in by asking a first question.

"At the time, were you satisfied with the conduct and conclusion of the investigation conducted by the police authorities?" Maximilien asked the Liverpools, who looked at each other uneasily. He took a risk and asked a more direct question. "Do you believe that Charlie Liverpool's death was accidental?"

Mrs. Liverpool broke down in tears, and her husband put his hand on her shoulder before looking at Maximilien. "We never accepted it. Charlie was a high-level athlete and was well aware of the dangers of sliding on the cliffs of the island. When he was young, he often accompanied me on fishing trips on Sundays. I took him to a cove that was a fifteen-minute walk from Castries. To get there, we had to climb some steep cliffs. He was aware of the dangers and always moved cautiously."

"And my son would never have voluntarily ended his life," Mrs. Liverpool added, somewhat recovering from her emotions.

Maximilien understood the pain he was causing this couple. He thought of his own son, Eric. However, he knew that parental love could sometimes blind one's perception and understanding of their own children. He had to continue his questioning. "Tell me about his life at that time—his activities, his associations, his friends, his joys and... If he had experienced any love pains."

Mr. Liverpool spoke first, saying that Charlie was very involved in the Caribbean Premier League cricket and the West Indies international team. He had a lot of difficulty dealing with his celebrity status as a member of Saint Lucia's famous trio, unlike his teammate Nigel Glenwood. Despite this, he was happy with his life as a cricket player. Mr. Liverpool had never sensed despair or resentment in him.

"And he had no enemies," he concluded, turning his gaze to his wife.

"He spent his entire youth in the sports parks with Nigel. They were inseparable. Charlie liked Nigel. He would come home for dinner and talk only about Nigel's athletic prowess."

"And what about female friends? Did he have any romantic relationships? Did he ever introduce a girlfriend to you?" Max asked them.

"No," Mrs. Liverpool replied after a few seconds of reflection.

They continued to divulge their confidences about their son. After a few minutes, Maximilien recognized that he had abused their patience enough by forcing them to relive painful memories. He looked over at Peter to see if he had a question. Peter gave him a negative sign.

"Thank you for your kindness, and I apologize for making you relive these difficult moments about Charlie," said Max.

"Yes, thank you for your cooperation," added Peter in a more official tone.

"Mr. Liverpool, would you consent to a DNA test between you and James Charles?" asked Max.

"I don't know. Do you think it's necessary?" he replied, a little incredulous.

"There is a test called intergenerational, done on two people to determine if they are related by genealogical DNA. This will confirm or refute the question of Charlie's paternity," said Max.

"I'm willing. Is it effective?"

"It would require me to take a few samples of your hair, specifically six strands of hair with the bulb or root. This will be enough to perform an effective and reliable DNA test," replied Maximilien.

Max proceeded with Mr. Liverpool's permission and asked Mrs. Liverpool for a Ziploc bag. Once he was done, he and Peter thanked them again and made their way down to the village. On the way, Max noticed that he had received a text message from Jessica informing him that she would be back at the Bel Jou and available from three o'clock onwards.

Once they were on their way back, Peter broke the silence that had settled since they had left the Liverpool's.

"Several things lead me to believe that Charlie is not James Charles's biological father!"

"I know, my friend. It's like we're in some kind of love triangle: Charlie, Nigel, and Jessica. Charlie's mother's comments about the strong friendship, not to mention the adoration that Charlie has for Nigel leaves me perplexed," said Max.

"You're referring to his sexual orientation?"

"I'm referring to everything, but that's not the issue. If we consider ruling out the accidental aspect and consider the hypothesis of murder, our main challenge is to identify the motive," replied Max.

"For both events?"

"Possibly, if we believe they're related. But the next step to clarify the situation is to perform the DNA test as quickly as possible."

Maximilien told Peter that he knew the director of a laboratory in Montreal who could perform this type of test quickly. He was a family friend. Max suggested that Peter go to the morgue to obtain a sample of James' DNA. Peter would then send the two samples by FedEx, on a priority basis, to the Montreal laboratory. Meanwhile, he would meet Jessica at the Bel Jou. Peter mentioned that the FedEx plane landed at the Castries airport every day around three o'clock, and then went on to Miami, from where packages were sent, among other places, to Toronto and Montreal. He estimated that it would take twenty-four hours for their package to reach Montreal.

"I will text you the name and address of the recipient, and I will notify him by phone later today," said Max.

"Okay," replied Peter.

Peter dropped Max off at the Bel Jou and went on to complete his shipping task. It was two forty-five p.m. The Bel Jou hotel, located on a rocky plateau overlooking Castries, was built into the mountainside. The location offered a complete view of the city, its harbor, and the Caribbean Sea.

Maximilien went to the reception and asked the attendant to inform Mrs. Jessica Charles of his presence. The employee checked the registration book and picked up the phone while asking Max to identify himself.

"Mrs. Charles!"

"Yes."

"Good morning, we have a Mr. Le Gardeur here to see you."

"Oh, so soon? Please have him seated on the pool terrace and tell him that I will join him in a few minutes."

"Okay, ma'am."

"Thank you."

The attendant conveyed the message to Max and signaled for a waiter to escort the guest to the terrace. They made him sit in the shade and asked if he would like a drink, which he refused. Maximilien examined the hotel complex, unable to doubt its four-star rating. The infinity pool at the front of the complex offered a panoramic view of the sea.

As soon as Jessica appeared at the end of the pool, walking toward the terrace, Maximilien and all the hotel guests sitting around the pool and terrace were captivated. All dressed in black, with a model's gait, she caught everyone's attention. She wore tight-fitting pants from the waist to the knees, but loose at the bottom, a light blouse, and a matching hat. She had on mid-high white heels and a wide white belt through the loops of her pants. Her slender feminine figure made it all elegant and sober.

Jessica had no trouble identifying her guest among the hotel guests. She removed her sunglasses and, approaching Max, extended her hand. Maximilien noticed her red eyes that did not diminish her beauty.

"Mr. Le Gardeur. Finally, I meet you in person, apart from yesterday at the funeral."

Max, still captivated, stood up and shook her hand.

"Hello and delighted to meet you, Mrs. Charles," Max replied, while pulling out the adjacent chair to invite her to sit.

"Please, call me Jessica."

"Okay, but only if you agree to call me Maximilien."

"Firstly, let me apologize again for alluding to the event regarding your son to convince you to accept my request for help."

"I beg of you; I am precisely in a position to understand you," he replied.

She signaled a waiter who hurriedly came to their table. Turning to Max, she asked, "Would you like to join me for some tea?"

"Of course!" he replied.

"We'll have your Darjeeling black tea for two, please," she told the waiter.

Jessica explained that she knew the owner's daughter of Bel Jou, a childhood friend. She had chosen to stay here instead of going to the *Golden Apple*.

"Please, tell me what you've learned. What do you have to say?" she eagerly asked him after they were served their tea.

"Firstly, let me say that the more I investigate, the more it all intrigues me. But first, let me tell you about what I've been up to since I arrived."

Maximilien gave her a report on the people he had met and questioned so far, while giving his general first impressions of each of them. When he mentioned the name Josephine Jackson, Maximilien noticed that Jessica seemed a little taken aback. He didn't mention his meeting with the Liverpool's, preferring to wait until the end of the conversation. Max explained that his investigation was mainly focused on her son's activities on the island during the two weeks before the tragedy, as well as, his quest to learn more about his family. Thus, he believed that he could potentially find answers to some of the questions raised during his initial interviews. Jessica listened without comment, looking perplexed.

"May I ask you a question about Charlie Liverpool, James' biological father?" Max asked.

"Of course."

"How did you cope with his accidental death, which happened twenty-one years ago?" he inquired.

"I loved him," Jessica admitted.

She said that that period had been painful for her. Charlie was the man she had always wanted as a partner, for life. He had everything—intelligence, kindness, sensitivity, and honesty. She had been shocked when she heard of his death.

"Is that the real reason you left Saint Lucia?" Max asked.

"No, it was really my pregnancy," she replied.

"This morning, just before coming to see you, I met Charlie's parents. They live in Micoud," he revealed.

"Oh really?" she said, surprised. "Why?"

"I don't want to insinuate anything at this stage of my

investigation, but some clues lead me to believe that there may be a connection between the tragic death of your son and Charlie's," he said.

Maximilien didn't reveal all the details he had gathered during that meeting and made no mention of the DNA test that would be conducted. He told her that Nigel Glenwood was supposed to land on the island tomorrow, and that he intended to question him. He noticed that this last comment seemed to unsettle her once again.

"Did you know that he is the owner of the *Golden Apple Inn*?" Max asked.

"No, you're telling me," Jessica replied.

They chatted for a few more minutes. Maximilien described the next steps in his investigation and they agreed to talk every day. This way, he would keep her informed of the progress of his investigation. Jessica expressed her desire to meet Julietta.

"My mother recommended that I have a conversation with her because of the relationship she had built with James during his stay at the *Golden Apple*," she said.

"I totally agree," Max replied.

"But you understand that I don't want to go to the inn," she added.

"Of course. I'll give her your number and ask her to contact you."

"That would be appreciated, thank you."

He left her, wishing her a good rest of the day.

Maximilien returned to the front desk and asked the attendant to call him a taxi. At the same time, Peter forwarded him a text confirming the shipment of the package to Montreal at the address Max had provided. He also provided him with the tracking number.

***

It was five thirty p.m. when he arrived at the *Golden Apple*. Charlie was still at the front desk. Maximilien asked him if he could use one of the inn's phone lines to make a call to Canada. Charlie nodded and confirmed that the phone booth's line was available.

"Hello!" Jules answered after a few rings.

"Hey, Jules. How are you?" Max asked.

"Hey, Max, are you calling me from abroad?"

"Yeah, I agreed to conduct an investigation in Saint Lucia."

"Saint Lucia in Florida?"

"No, in the Caribbean. Listen, I have a favor to ask you."

Maximilien explained the main lines of his investigation and asked if he could perform a fast-track genealogical DNA test between the victim and her presumed biological grandfather. His friend grudgingly accepted, stipulating that he wouldn't be able to do the job before tomorrow evening.

"I'll be out tomorrow, giving a lecture in Trois-Rivières," Jules explained.

"No problem, the package should arrive tomorrow in the late afternoon," Maximilien replied, communicating the tracking number and thanking Jules. Jules promised to send him a text message as soon as he had the results.

"Thanks," Max said to Charlie when he returned to the reception.

"Mr. Le Gardeur, I regret to inform you that the dining room is not open tonight. Annetta hasn't returned, and I couldn't reach her assistant, Justin," Charlie informed him.

"Oh, really?"

"There are a few restaurants nearby that we have agreements with, like KFC or Domino's Pizza. Here's a coupon for eighty Eastern Caribbean dollars, courtesy of the house."

"Thank you. Does that mean I can't order a gin and tonic?" Max asked.

"No, but since I'm alone tonight, I'll go and prepare it and bring it to your room," Charlie replied.

Max smiled gratefully and headed to his room. Charlie placed a sign on the counter that read, "Back soon, thank you," and left for the dining room bar.

A few minutes later, there was a knock on Maximilien's door. It was Charlie, who came in and set down a tray containing two gin and tonics, a small bucket of ice, and a plate of lime slices.

"There you go! I brought you two drinks and the ice separately so you can add it to your drink as you please. Enjoy your evening," Charlie said.

Max thanked him and slipped him a tip. He took a shower, changed clothes, and went to sit on the patio to smoke a good cigar. It had been five days since he had arrived on the island. What had he accomplished? He admitted to himself that every piece of information he obtained raised new questions. Was he on the right track in linking the accidental death of Charlie Liverpool and, twenty-one years later, that of James Charles? He went to fetch his second gin and tonic.

Half an hour had passed since the darkness of the night had set in. *I'm hungry*, he thought. He grabbed his nylon jacket, coupon, and left his room. Passing by the reception, he mentioned to Charlie that he would try the Domino's Pizza restaurant.

"You go up to the main road. It's a five-minute walk to the right, and you can't miss it," Charlie said. "Do you have your coupon?"

Maximilien nodded and began his walk. Traffic was slow on the main road, especially from Castries toward Gros-Islet. He saw the bright sign of Domino's Pizza and entered. He noticed a few tables near the large window, offering a view of the road, where a string of cars moved slowly, leaving its share of carbon monoxide in the air. He thought of eating in, but quickly opted for takeout. He chose the classic Lucian pizza with two Piton beers.

With his meal in hand, Max walked down the small street leading to the inn. He stopped in front of the Glenwood house, hoping to see Clinton. All the lights in the house were off, so he continued on his way. He decided to take the path through the garden of small flowering shrubs to his room, number 12.

As he approached, he saw a human figure near his patio. "Is that one of the inn's guests?" he wondered. Being in the low season, the inn had few tenants. Max had noticed a young woman and an elderly couple, who were currently guests at the inn. He advanced further and noticed that it was a man carrying a box. His level of suspicion rose when he realized that the individual was heading toward his patio door. As he was about to slide it open, Max decided to intervene.

"Hey, my friend, can I help you?"

The man, surprised, turned around and, seeing Max, threw the box at him, hitting him on the left shoulder. Upon contact, Max heard a sound coming from inside the box, a sort of whistling noise. He pushed the object toward the ground with his arm, as he dropped his dinner bag and, realizing that the intruder was trying to escape, he jumped toward him to catch him by the legs. The intruder fell, but turned around to elbow

Max in the face. While Max absorbed the shock, his attacker tried to get up, but Max got up just as quickly. He grabbed the man's shoulder to turn him over and punched him in the face, followed by another punch to the abdomen. It was his turn to make sounds of pain.

As Max was immobilizing him on the ground, the man shouted, "Charlie! Charlie! Come and help me."

Maximilien put him in an arm lock, causing unbearable pain, which he understood from the scream that followed. He looked around him, imagining another man named Charlie coming to attack him.

"I'm warning you; I'll break your arm if you try to escape," Max said as he guided him into his room.

Once inside, Max immobilized him once again on the ground and reached for his suitcase with his other hand to take out handcuffs. He always carried this tool when he traveled. Once the man was handcuffed, he went outside to check the contents of the box. He approached it cautiously, remembering the whistling sound. He turned it over and saw the creature escape into the gardens. He quickly stepped back, realizing it was a snake.

He went back inside and immediately called his friend Peter. Once he confirmed that he would be there in about ten minutes, he made sure his prisoner was securely tied up and went to the reception, where there was no one. He headed to the dining room, where no one was either. Was the Charlie the handcuffed man had called for the same Charlie at the reception? He went outside and shouted "Charlie" a few times. He was gone.

Peter arrived and the two of them headed toward the bedroom. Once they got there, Max leaned over to turn over the intruder who was lying face down.

"Danny," Peter exclaimed in consternation.

"Do you know this person?" Max asked.

"Yes, it's the deputy commander of the police station, Danny Ford," replied Peter.

Chapter 06

Wednesday, May 11, 2005

The alarm clock rang, and Max got out of bed as soon as he realized that his night was over. So many things and facts were swirling in his head. He looked at his watch, it was seven-thirty. He was surprised that he had managed to sleep for several hours despite the events of the previous day.

The evening before, after Maximilien had described everything that had happened since his return from the Domino's Pizza restaurant to Peter, the latter had contacted the police station to have them send a car to pick up the number one suspect in the attack. In the meantime, Peter had tried to question Danny without success; he remained as silent as a fish. As for Charlie, Peter had informed Max that the next day, a search warrant would be issued and sent to all police stations in Saint Lucia.

"You will have to go to the police station tomorrow to make an official statement," Peter had told Max.

"Absolutely, and I want to have a meeting with Commander Simpson."

"Okay. I will also contact the reptile conservation agency to explain the situation to them and hopefully they can come and capture the reptile. I don't like knowing that it's roaming free in a residential area."

Peter had left Max, wishing him a good night's sleep and

assuring him that an officer would be stationed at the entrance of the hotel all night.

***

Max quickly finished his morning toilette and got dressed. He immediately headed toward the reception of the inn while pondering over recent events.

How to summarize the situation? An assassination attempt on his life, similar to the James Charles' case, had taken place the previous day. The intruder, Danny Ford, was none other than the deputy commander of the Sainte-Lucie police station and the third member of the infamous Fer de Lance trio. Charlie Roy, the assistant manager of the *Golden Apple Inn*, was apparently his accomplice. Now, a venomous snake was freely circulating in the Marisule district.

First observation, both James Charles' search in Sainte-Lucie and Maximilien's investigation into his death had triggered the same action from a frustrated and fearful individual. Second observation, there was likely a link between the death of young Charles and the fatal accident of his biological father, Charlie Liverpool.

What had really happened twenty-one years ago? What motives lay behind all these events? Love, money, honor? Why had Danny Ford attempted to take Maximilien Le Gardeur's life? Was he the one who had introduced Fer de Lance into James Charles' room? Who was the mastermind behind it, if there was one?

When Max arrived at the reception, JJ was talking to the security guard. Upon seeing Maximilien, she walked over to him.

"Ah, Monsieur Le Gardeur, poor you! I am sorry. I just learned what happened yesterday. How are you doing?" she asked.

"I'm okay, thank you," replied Max. "Your assistant disappeared last night."

"What are you saying? I don't understand," JJ said, confused.

Realizing that Josephine did not have all the details of the incident from the previous day, Maximilien revealed the probable involvement of Charlie Roy in the attack, and his escape when he realized the operation was failing. JJ was completely stunned by these revelations.

"Despite his nonchalance and indifferent air, I never thought he could be involved in this kind of plot. Nigel will be surprised," she said.

"Why?" Max asked.

"They are childhood friends. Nigel asked me to hire him for a position at the inn."

"Recently?"

"No, it's been ten years and he's never caused any problems other than being a bit moody."

Josephine continued, mentioning that she was looking forward to the arrival of the owner, Nigel Glenwood, later that afternoon. She informed Maximilien that there would be a lot of commotion around the inn and apologized in advance for any inconvenience it would cause during his stay. She reassured him that Commander Simpson would arrange, as usual for any of Nigel's visits to Sainte-Lucie, to assign security agents to establish a secure perimeter around the inn.

"Really? To that extent?" Max exclaimed, incredulous.

"You'll see for yourself," she replied.

Max thanked her and headed toward the dining room. As soon as he was seated at one of the tables, he saw outside, near the banana garden, a man holding a box in one hand and an instrument in the other. He was talking to Oscar, the gardener. The box, with its shape and color, caught his attention. It took him a few seconds to realize that it was similar to the one that the intruder had thrown at him the previous day. He went back to his room to check. Max slid open his patio door. The box was still there and, indeed, it was the same. He retrieved it and placed it in his room.

Max decided to go and meet the two men near the banana trees. They were still talking when Max intervened, "Good morning, gentlemen."

"Be careful, don't come any closer," Oscar warned him, using his forearm as a barrier.

Max froze.

Early in the morning, when Oscar had learned of the events of the previous day, he was convinced that he knew where the Kravat had taken refuge. Yesterday evening, he had scraped the banana garden and formed a pile of banana leaves, which he intended to collect today.

"The Fer de Lance is in the area and Oscar believes that the frightened reptile has hidden in his pile of banana leaves," Willie mentioned.

"I see... And who are you?" Max asked him.

"My name is Willie Norris; I work for the reptile conservation agency of Saint Lucia."

He explained to Max that the Fer de Lance preferred the moisture created by banana leaves resting on the ground. They liked to sneak in and wait for the Anolis to descend, their favorite food. The Anolis was a small lizard that could be found on banana trees and only came down to the ground to feed. Unfortunately, it thus became the prey of the Fer de Lance. That is why the Kravat represented the greatest threat to agricultural workers in banana plantations.

"You see these boots?" he added, pointing to his feet. "They were designed for banana plantation workers. The rubber is three times thicker and the shoe goes up to the knees."

"And this box is it used for capturing the Fer de Lance?" Max asked.

"Not necessarily, but I make it considering the characteristics of the Fer de Lance, its strength, and its agility. It only exists on the island of Saint Lucia."

"You're the designer and I presume you're the only one who uses them," Max commented.

Willie hesitated to agree with Max's last comment. Oscar, who was rather in the background, approached them to indicate to Willie that it was time to intervene before the Kravat decided to change location.

"Good luck. Maybe, you should call a mongoose," Max said candidly.

His remark caused a look of horror on the faces of the two men. They looked at each other and, without saying a word, turned around to enter the banana garden. Max, preferring to let them work, returned to the dining room.

As planned, Peter arrived at the inn at nine o'clock. Max got into the car, and Peter shifted into first gear to head in the direction of the police station. On the way, Peter told Max that the tension was palpable at the police station now that the deputy commander was behind bars. He also mentioned that he had gotten his hands on all the newspaper articles from the time regarding the tragic death of the cricket player Charlie Liverpool.

"I thought you would like to read these articles. They contain information that helps better understand the circumstances surrounding the player's death," said Peter.

"Definitely, my friend. You did well," replied Max.

In turn, Max described to Peter his conversation with the reptile conservation agency attendant, Willie Norris. He told him about the great similarity between the box used by his attacker the night before and the one used by the attendant who was trying to capture the Fer-de-Lance.

"I would like to question him. Could you arrange a meeting, ideally at the conservation agency?" asked Max.

"Certainly," replied Peter.

They arrived at the police station. Peter took Max to the closed office where depositions were taken. He opened the computer and displayed the template containing the basic questions. After recording the identity of the deponent, Maximilien's chronological testimony was taken. As he detailed the events that had happened the previous day, Max, who was reliving the scene in his head, couldn't help but think of the night when young James Charles had died after being bitten by a venomous snake.

The conversation he had with Charlie Roy at the reception the night before came to mind. The attendant had been nervous and had answered a little too quickly when asked about the exact time James had left the inn to get himself a meal. Of course, he was in cahoots with Danny, his attacker, but who had ordered this act? His thoughts were interrupted by someone bursting into the room.

"Monsieur Le Gardeur, I am extremely sorry about this

incident, what a mishap! I will personally participate in the investigation," said Commander Simpson.

"Commander Simpson, that is your prerogative, but the facts are that you can no longer ignore the obvious links between the murder of James Charles and the tragic death of his biological father, Charlie Liverpool," replied Max.

Clearly annoyed, Hercule Simpson pulled up a chair to sit facing Maximilien.

"Monsieur Le Gardeur, do I need to remind you that the investigation and the coroner's report concerning young James concluded that it was an accidental death? I'm happy to respect the mandate you received from Mrs. Charles, but I repeat that your findings will have no impact in our jurisdiction, on my island," he said, sitting up straight with his chest puffed out.

"The theory of an accidental death often comes up in your investigations, don't you think?" asked Max.

"I have to leave for the airport," said Hercule, ignoring Max's last comment.

"I'd like to continue our conversation. Do you have any free time this afternoon?" asked Max.

"Impossible, today and tomorrow, I have to oversee everything related to Nigel Glenwood's arrival in Saint Lucia," replied Hercule.

"The return of the prodigal son! My request for an interview stands. I'll check with your office for your availability in the coming days," said Max.

"Okay," Hercule simply replied, getting up to leave the room.

Maximilien did not appreciate the conversation and did not understand why the commander was so indifferent toward his investigation. Peter was uncomfortable, caught between a rock and a hard place: his participation in Maximilien's investigation and his loyalty to his boss. He finished entering Max's statement into the system, and then showed him some newspaper articles about the tragic death of cricket player Charlie Liverpool.

Max noted that the idea of love, sorrow, often appeared in the different articles, as well as, the victim's emotional instability. However, they all expressed doubts about the accidental aspect of the tragedy at the secret creek promontory.

"I would like to visit this promontory," Max said. "Is it still accessible?"

"Yes, we have to go around the airport, it's located at the tip of Vigie," Peter replied.

"Then let's go."

As they were about to leave the room, a man entered. Maximilien didn't know him. Albert Monfils, the chief coroner, introduced himself and expressed his pleasure at finally meeting Major Maximilien Le Gardeur.

"We crossed paths at the funeral of young James Charles without having the chance to introduce ourselves to each other," Albert said.

"Yes, your face looks familiar," Max replied.

"I was just informed about the attack on your life. Rest assured that I intend to closely follow this case," said Albert.

"There is definitely someone on the island who feels threatened by my presence," said Maximilien.

"How is your investigation going, if you don't mind me asking?" the coroner asked.

Maximilien shared the main points and, realizing that his interlocutor was showing honest and professional interest, decided to confide his hypotheses about the links between the death of young James Charles and that of his alleged biological father, Charlie Liverpool. He did not reveal all the details that he had not yet managed to link together himself, but he had already imagined some scenarios.

"Interesting. Know that you can count on my support for the rest of your investigation. Don't hesitate to contact me if there is any obstruction to your work," added Albert Monfils.

Max thanked him and the coroner left the room. The two men followed him closely to go to the secret creek promontory. As mentioned by Peter, from Castries, one had to leave the city from the north, go around the national airport runway and go along the cemetery, where young Charles had been buried.

The promontory was located at the end of the Vigie peninsula. The peninsula, with its elevation and its view toward Martinique, constituted the strategic location for a watchtower. In fact, it was on this peninsula that the British had erected most of their military and command buildings in the 19th century.

Peter drove his car as far as possible on the path leading to the promontory and parked it in the shade of a tree. As soon as he got out of the car, Max noticed the tree in question. It was huge, both in height and girth, with a slender frame that ended in a spread of leafy branches, like a large parasol that could shade two tennis courts.

"Impressive. Surely the emblematic tree of Saint Lucia," he dared to advance.

"For some, it is, because it is unique on the island, but the two official emblematic trees of Saint Lucia are the cherry and the calabash tree," Peter replied.

"This one is from the almond family, but here on the island, it can reach twenty meters and be over a hundred years old."

They took a beaten path for two hundred meters to reach

the extreme tip of the peninsula. There was a clear and steep area and an old protective stone wall, built in the last century. The promontory offered an unobstructed view of the ocean horizon. Peter explained to Max that history told of how in the 19th century, the wives of British naval officers came here every day to scan the horizon hoping to see a ship flying the British flag. Their fear, in the absence of their husbands, was to see a ship with a French flag or one bearing the likeness of pirates hoisted on the mast.

"Today, the place is used for love declarations and marriage proposals of young Saint Lucians," Peter mentioned.

Examining the surroundings, Maximilien realized that a fall at this location must have been intentional or provoked, whether by an altercation or intent of homicide. Imagining a confrontation between two individuals, he deduced that the height of the wall could not prevent a person from tipping over and crashing onto the reefs. The escarpment had a seventy-five-foot drop at low tide.

"Do you arrive at the same conclusion as me?" Max asked Peter.

"The accidental dimension is difficult to conceive," Peter replied.

"Exactly, my friend."

They turned back. As soon as he returned to the car, Maximilien sent a text message to Jessica Charles:

"Hello, I'm presently in Castries. Can I be dropped off at your hotel to see you?"

He received a prompt reply, "Hello, Mr. Le Gardeur. Sorry, we'll have to postpone this to tomorrow. I'm currently at my parent's in Choiseul. I should be back in Castries tomorrow early afternoon."

"Okay, have a good evening," he replied.

They arrived at the descending road leading to the *Golden Apple Inn*. Peter had to stop his car quickly after entering it. There were a lot of people blocking it while others were on the grounds adjacent to the inn, mostly young people. With the sound of his horn, he managed to make his way to the inn's gate. A security agent approached the vehicle and, after recognizing Peter, immediately opened the entrance gate. The agent and one of his colleagues had to restrain the crowd and prevent them from entering while Peter's car crossed the gate.

"I had been warned about this kind of gathering," Max said.

"Yes, Nigel is in town, and everyone wants to see him and get an autograph or just a look from him."

Peter left Max in the inn's parking lot.

"You'll have to go through that crowd again, I'm sorry," Max said.

"Don't worry about it. Have a good rest of the day. I'll wait for your call regarding the schedule for tomorrow."

As Peter made his way to the gate, Maximilien entered the reception of the inn. To his surprise, he found Amanda behind the reception desk!

"Hello, Monsieur Le Gardeur!" greeted Amanda.

"Hello, Amanda! I'm surprised to see you here," replied Max.

"JJ offered me the position of assistant manager. It was perfect for me considering my studies, so I accepted," explained Amanda.

"Congratulations!" Max replied.

"Thank you!"

"It's crazy outside. When is the famous Nigel Glenwood

arriving?" Max asked.

"Very soon, according to the head of security. Oh yes, someone from Montreal was trying to reach you, a Mr. Jules. He left his phone number," Amanda informed him, handing him a small card with the inn's letterhead. "You can use the telephone booth in the small lounge if you want to call him back."

"Thanks, I would like that," Max replied.

"I'll transfer the call to the inn's line. Do you know how to signal a call to Canada?" she asked him.

He nodded and headed toward the small lounge. He entered the booth and dialed the series of numbers. After the fourth ring, a voice answered. "Hello, Maximilien?"

"Yes, hi Jules. How are you?" Max asked.

"Very well, thank you. And you, everything okay?" Jules replied.

"Yes, except for an assassination attempt on my life. But don't worry. Do you have any results to report?" Max inquired.

"Yes, the general relationship test came back negative," Jules announced.

"What? There's no genetic link between the two samples? Are you sure?" Max asked, incredulous.

Jules explained that the DNA test to establish an intergenerational parental relationship was effective and reliable. He confirmed that he had checked the data and was one hundred per cent convinced of the result confirming that Charlie Liverpool was not James Charles's biological father. This disturbed all the scenarios imagined by Maximilien.

"I'm sorry if the results contradict your hypotheses," Jules said.

"Don't worry, my friend, it reinforces some other

indicators. I'll have to redirect my research leads," Max replied.

"The assassination attempt worries me, be careful. Don't forget that you'll be a grandfather in a few months," Jules reminded him.

"What? What are you talking about?" Max exclaimed, not quite understanding.

"France is pregnant, didn't you know?" Jules informed him.

Max's body struggled to absorb the strong emotion caused by this news. A syncope invaded his body; all the psychedelic drugs he had consumed recently seemed to rise up his nervous system to his brain like effluvium. He barely had time to straighten up from his stool when his hand dropped the receiver, as he lost consciousness. He collapsed against the door of the booth and fell to the ground in the small lounge.

***

Quebec, Quebec Three Months Earlier,
Friday, February 11, 2005

That day, Maximilien had his bi-monthly appointment with his psychologist. He had been seeing him for several years, ever since the death of his son Eric, in fact, when the relational barriers with his daughter France had arisen. His daughter accused him of her brother's death and held him responsible for her difficulty to get pregnant. This pain, this sense of guilt, plunged him into depression and increased his anxiety. All conventional psychological treatments had failed to reduce his stress and the depression that plagued him. On that day, his psychologist offered him a new treatment recently approved on an experimental basis by the health authorities: psychedelic drugs to support psychological treatments.

"The treatment involves taking micro doses of LSD. These pills work similarly to anti-depressants, it's a biological mechanism," the psychologist explained.

"I've never taken drugs! I don't want to become dependent!" protested the patient.

"Don't worry, there are no side effects. We only use micro doses," the psychologist reassured his patient. "Your problem is your relationship with your pain. You can't seem to get out of your guilt syndrome."

The psychologist explained that this form of therapy aimed to change the meaning the patient gave to his pain so that it would no longer plunge him into depression and decrease his anxiety. The neurons affected by LSD stimulated the serotonin and dopamine cycle, and acted like a neuromodulator that facilitated communication between neurons. It was like circumventing a psychological phenomenon called dissociation, where the patient refused to think about certain painful questions and see themselves from the outside.

"You must change your perception of your psychological issue and realize that you are not responsible for your daughter's infertility," the psychologist continued to convince his patient.

Maximilien complied and began the treatment at his next visit. He was on his fourth treatment when he agreed to go to the Caribbean at Jessica Charles' request.

***

Amanda, from her position at the reception desk, heard the loud noise coming from the small lounge. Accompanied by a few people present in the vestibule, she rushed into the adjacent room.

With the help of a man, she leaned over to lift Max's body and asked for a towel soaked in cold water.

"Clear the area, he needs more air," the man holding Max said as he placed the towel on his forehead.

Max was slowly beginning to regain his senses. Amanda could hear a voice calling out, "Max, Max." She picked up the phone.

"Hello..."

"What's going on? Is Max okay?" Jules asked.

"It seems he had a weakness, but now he's getting better," Amanda replied.

At the very beginning, Max, who was regaining his senses, recognized the small lounge even though his vision was a bit blurry. He saw a man leaning over him, but he didn't know who he was.

"Who are you?" he asked.

"My name is Nigel, Nigel Glenwood."

Chapter 07

Thursday, May 12, 2005

It had been another restless night for Maximilien. Despite that, when he woke up, he still had the same smile on his face from the previous day. His daughter, who had tried to reach him the previous Friday, had probably wanted to tell him that she was pregnant. It lifted a negative weight off his mind.

But that joy was not the only thing occupying his thoughts that morning. Although he was not completely surprised by the DNA test results, it added another layer of complexity to his investigation. Nigel Glenwood had become a witness who could help him with the next steps. Last night, after Max had regained his composure and thanked his rescuers, Nigel had invited him for breakfast in his suite. The inspector had accepted.

All the rooms in the inn were similar, except for the one called the owner's suite. Located at the end of the hallway on the second floor, it had a living room, a walk-in shower, and a large balcony. The appointment was set for nine o'clock. Max looked at his watch and decided to take a shower. He left his room around eight fifty.

"Good morning, please come in," said Nigel.

"Thank you," said Maximilien.

Nigel invited him to follow him. They crossed the living room, and he opened the patio door to the balcony. Annetta was setting the table there. Max greeted her, but she remained silent.

Breakfast was served, a large plate of fruit, bake, soft-boiled eggs, and cold meats.

"Orange juice or coffee?" Nigel asked.

"Orange juice to start would be appreciated," replied Max.

Nigel thanked Annetta, and the two men took their seats. At this time of day, the terrace was completely in the shade, which Maximilien noticed and appreciated. Already, several young Saint Lucians had gathered at the inn's gate, and they could hear them chanting "Nigel, Nigel, Nigel" whenever they sensed movement at the entrance of the *Golden Apple*.

"How are you feeling this morning? Have you recovered from yesterday's events?" Nigel asked immediately.

"Fully recovered, thank you," replied Max.

"I apologize for the attack, but I am also puzzled by this incident at my inn. The commander himself has entrusted me with taking care of the investigation. Rest assured that you are now safe here at the *Golden Apple*."

"I am, now, thanks to your presence," added Max with a hint of sarcasm.

"I'm glad my presence reassures you," he replied, quick-wittedly and with a touch of derision.

The conversation was established, but its content remained courteous and friendly. After all, Nigel was a gentleman, a good host who had assimilated British composure. He was tall and athletically built, and his imposing jaw contributed to his charm when he smiled.

"Why did you leave Saint Lucia for England and these people who adore you?" Max asked.

Nigel greeted the question with a frown. How many times had he had to answer it? He explained that after the West Indies team's victory in the World Championship, he had continued his cricket career with the Saint Lucia national team. His manager at the time, a Briton, had advised him to exile himself to Great Britain in order to obtain dual citizenship, Saint Lucian and British. Obtaining British citizenship for island citizens was facilitated by a clause in the 1979 declaration of independence between England and Saint Lucia. Immigrating allowed him to join the England national cricket team and greatly increased his sponsorship opportunities. So, he went for it.

"Did you know Jessica Charles, the mother of the young victim, James Charles?" Max asked.

"Yes, but it wasn't until recently that I was informed of the link between the victim and Jessica. Like everyone else at the time, I was surprised by her mysterious disappearance from the island," Nigel replied.

"Let's get back to the young victim, James Charles. Why do you think he checked into your inn under the name James Charles Liverpool?"

"I have no idea, honestly."

"He claimed that his biological father was Charlie Liverpool and that he wanted to know the truth about his alleged accidental death at the time," Max said, while observing Nigel's non-verbal reaction.

He saw a great deal of emotional control in him. Nigel candidly repeated what he had heard from Josephine, the manager of his establishment. He confirmed to Maximilien that Charlie and he had been great childhood friends, that they had done everything together, school, mischief, and sports, naturally.

"And girls..." Maximilien continued.

Max immediately noticed that his last comment had caused a change in his host's attitude. His body language communicated discomfort, making it difficult for him to maintain his British composure. Nigel mumbled a few words indicating that, like all teenagers, it was part of their youth learning process.

"Like all teenage friends, you must have quarreled over the same girl at some point?"

Definitely annoyed by this question and seeking to change the course of the discussion, Nigel asked him how his investigation was going. Max thought it would be good to reveal some of his observations and thoughts, including the potential link between Charlie and young James's accidental deaths. He even confided that he doubted Charlie was James's biological father without revealing the DNA test results received the night before.

"I assume you didn't know that Jessica Charles had established herself in England following her mysterious disappearance from Saint Lucia," Maximilien asked him.

"No, not at all," Nigel replied.

"May I ask you an indiscreet question?"

"Of course, if I can answer it."

"Did you date Jessica Charles before she disappeared from the island?"

"You know, the Jessica of the time was the most coveted girl on the island, and beyond after her Miss West Indies coronation. So, yes, I tried to seduce her several times," he replied, without specifying whether his advances had been successful.

As Max was about to pursue this line of questioning, his cellphone beeped indicating the entry of a text. Immediately, Nigel, seeking to change the subject, asked him to take a look. The text came from Peter: "Good morning, I've arranged a meeting with Willie Norris for today at eleven o'clock. If it's okay with you, I'll pick you up at the inn around ten."

Max confirmed by replying: "OK."

Nigel had taken advantage of the break to leave the table and attend to some errands.

"Everything okay?" he asked Maximilien, as he took his seat again at the table.

"Yes, thank you. I was notified of a meeting at eleven o'clock with the head of the reptile preservation agency in Saint Lucia, a certain Willie Norris. Do you know him?"

"Willie? Of course, he was part of the maintenance management team for the Saint Lucian national team back in the day."

"So, Commander Hercule Simpson and he know each other very well," Max continued.

"Yes. However, I don't know if they still interact today," Nigel replied.

This exchange led Maximilien to mention the names of Danny Ford and Charlie Roy.

"What was your reaction upon learning that one of your cricket comrades, a member of the famous Fer de Lance trio, attempted to take my life?" Max asked.

"If you don't mind, I prefer not to answer that question and let the investigation continue," Nigel responded, visibly shaken by the fact.

"And Charlie Roy, his apparent accomplice whom you knew according to the information I obtained?" Max added.

"Likewise," Nigel replied, casting a vexed look at Maximilien.

The two men finished their breakfast and the conversation turned to more trivial matters. Before leaving, Maximilien informed Nigel that he would be meeting Jessica again at Bel Jou in the late afternoon.

"Tell her that I would like to see her to pay my respects and offer my condolences," Nigel said.

"I will gladly deliver the message. Know that she is still an attractive woman," Max replied.

The two men parted ways with a handshake, and Nigel indicated that he was available if his cooperation was needed in the investigation. Max headed to his room to prepare to go to the preservation agency.

***

To get to the preservation agency, one had to head toward Choiseul from Castries and, halfway there, turn toward the mountains.

"I presume you trust your friend from Montreal," Peter said after Max shared the DNA test results with him.

"Completely!"

"This reinforces our suspicions regarding Charlie Liverpool. But who the hell could be the father?" Peter exclaimed in surprise.

"Knowing that would help us set up the next stage of our investigation," Max replied.

"All of this brings us back to the famous love triangle of Charlie, Nigel, and Jessica," Peter said.

"I tried to broach the subject during breakfast with Nigel, but without success. He didn't commit himself. I have to meet with Jessica later, so we'll see how she reacts. Actually, I should text her. What time do you think we'll be back in Castries?" Max asked.

"I would say around three in the afternoon," Peter replied.

The gravel secondary road to the preservation agency had a thirty-five percent incline. In addition, on the flat parts of the road, Peter had to maneuver to avoid large potholes or rocks emerging from the ground. Maximilien held tightly to his seat.

"We're here!" exclaimed Peter.

"Finally!" cried Max.

Willie was waiting for them outside the building. After the customary greetings, he invited them inside. As soon as Maximilien entered, he recognized a scent he had smelled recently, the smell of old, smoky wood. Quickly, he made the connection to the old church in Castries. The former French garrison building, dating back to the early 1800s, still had its skeletal wooden structure from that time. Only a huge ceiling fan with bamboo blades turned slowly to provide some air circulation. Willie explained that this suited his tenants well.

"Thank you for agreeing to meet with us, Willie," said Peter. "As mentioned, Monsieur Le Gardeur is investigating the death of young James Charles at the *Golden Apple Inn* earlier this month. He would like to ask you some questions about it."

"No problem," he replied, turning to Max.

"Thank you, I'll be brief," began the investigator. "On the day the victim was discovered, according to the investigation report, you arrived on the scene thirty minutes after Commander Simpson. That seems quick. Where were you when you received the police call?"

"Um... let me remember. Oh yes, I was in Castries, at my cousin's."

"So, ten to fifteen minutes later, you arrive already equipped to catch the Fer-de-Lance snake?"

"Uh... Yes," he replied, tilting his head as his gaze

wandered from Max to Peter.

"It seems like you were expecting this call," Max said, while scrutinizing his body language.

Willie nervously chuckled before mentioning that he was always prepared for any eventuality. Max continued by asking him to repeat the contents of the phone call between him and the police that morning. Did he know, before arriving on the scene, that it was a Fer-de-Lance? And what happened to the captured snake? Maximilien noted some discomfort in his interlocutor. At the last question, Willie hesitated before confirming that the snake had been released into the wild.

"So, now it's at the mercy of the mongooses," Max said.

Willie did not respond, frozen by the comment. Maximilien continued by talking to him about the famous box for transporting captured reptiles.

"You say you designed this special box. Are you the only one who makes it on the island?"

"I believe so."

"Have you received any orders for your box recently?" Max asked.

"Am I being accused?" Willie asked somewhat annoyed, turning to Peter.

"No," Peter replied to reassure him.

"You worked with Commander Simpson on the Saint Lucia national cricket team, according to my research," Max said.

Willie nonchalantly nodded. Maximilien signaled to Peter with a look that he had no more questions. Peter thanked the host, and the two men returned to the car. It was only once they were on the main road heading toward Castries that they discussed the interrogation of Willie.

"You seemed to doubt his answers," Peter said.

"I wouldn't say he's guilty, but he seems to be hiding something. My problem is that I'm accumulating information, data, but if I can't identify the motive, I can't complete the puzzle."

"I noticed you mentioned the word mongoose, and that shook him up a bit," Peter added.

"It was intentional. I am starting to believe that the character on the island nicknamed 'the mongoose' exists and that he would have an influence on individuals, somewhat like the former director of the FBI in the sixties, John Edgar Hoover."

"You're referring to the American movie: *The Private Files of J. Edgar Hoover*."

"Exactly!"

***

At the beginning of the summer season, the Bel Jou hotel was not fully booked. As early as the end of April, the tourist traffic to Saint Lucia would drop by fifty percent, only to pick up again in mid-November.

Jessica had arranged to meet Julietta at the Bel Jou in the afternoon. She had finished her shift at the *Golden Apple Inn* earlier that day. The two women were seated on the pool terrace.

"It's nice of you to meet with me, Julietta."

"I have to admit it makes me a bit uncomfortable. My mother told me about you. She said you were a beautiful woman, and that you suddenly disappeared from the island without explanation. Why?"

"It's too complicated. It doesn't matter anymore. Today, I

want to talk about James. I've heard that you were very close to him during his stay at the inn. I'd like to hear about the kind of interactions you had with my son," she said, looking very fondly at the young woman.

Julietta leaned back in her chair and sighed wistfully. She revealed that she had fallen in love with James the first day their eyes met and expressed what had attracted her to him; his presence, his kindness, his beauty, and especially his honesty and elegance. Jessica, the mother, drank in her words. She could feel that Julietta had loved her son.

"He was so happy to have met his grandparents," said Julietta. "But he was frustrated about his search for his father. Were you in love with Charlie Liverpool?" she asked in amazement.

"Yes," Jessica replied dreamily.

Meanwhile, a hotel staff member approached their table to inform Jessica that a Mr. Le Gardeur was at the reception desk and wished to see her.

"We'll have to continue our conversation another time," she said to Julietta. "But I insist!"

"No problem," she replied.

Jessica asked the staff member to bring her new guest to their table on the terrace. Julietta decided to wait for his arrival before leaving.

"Hello, ladies," said Maximilien. "I see I'm arriving at a bad time."

"No, I was just leaving," said Julietta.

"Hello, Maximilien. Please, take a seat," added Jessica.

The three chatted for a few minutes, and then Julietta left. Immediately, Jessica asked Max for the latest news on the investigation. What a surprise it was for her to learn of

Maximilien's attack! She asked him to end the investigation.

"I've lost my son, and I couldn't bear for someone else to suffer the same fate while trying to solve his death," she said.

"I understand and respect your wishes, but I've reached the point of no return in my investigation."

"Not at the risk of your life," she insisted.

"Don't worry, I don't intend to die. After all, I'll be a grandfather in a few months," he said with a proud smile.

"Congratulations... I won't have that chance," she replied with a hint of sadness in her voice.

"All the more reason to let me continue my investigation. You owe it to him."

Maximilien made reference to the tragic death of his own son. He assured her that she could not find inner peace until the truth surrounding James' death was known. At the very least, they needed to do everything possible to try and reveal it to the public.

"But for that, I need your help. You owe it to me to be transparent, to tell me the truth," he said to Jessica.

Jessica looked at him, communicating an attitude of collaboration, but Max sensed that her shell was not ready to fully open. He decided to be direct.

"I'll be honest with you, I don't believe that Charlie Liverpool is James' biological father," he said.

"But... what are you saying? Are you insinuating that I lied to you? Honestly..."

Maximilien offered her a compassionate and open look, giving her time to reflect. Jessica's gaze roamed around, seeking references that would allow her to counter Max's assertion. She didn't find any, and she broke down in tears.

"I... I don't understand... I loved him, I gave him my

love... and then, coldly, he told me that he didn't want me, but someone else. He never wanted to reveal the name of this lover," she sighed.

Maximilien said nothing, waiting for other comments, other confidences.

"All men desired me... You know, I was a beautiful woman," she said sadly.

"I have no doubt about that," Max simply replied. "Is that the last time you saw him alive?"

"Yes, his body was found three days later. It saddened me a lot, but the fact that he rejected me helped me in my mourning... It eased my pain, you understand," she asked Maximilien, seeking his indulgence.

"The investigation indicated an accidental death. Did that surprise you?"

"Very much... But I didn't try to find out more."

"In our first meeting, you mentioned that the reason for your secret departure from the island was not related to Charlie's death, but rather to hide your pregnancy from your parents and the community of Castries."

"Exactly!"

"What about the true biological father of James Charles?" Max asked.

She recoiled in her seat. Maximilien felt her shell closing again. He asked the question again.

"Who is the true father of James Charles?"

She looked at him while thinking about what she should answer. Her discomfort made her retreat even further in her seat, displaying the look of a hunted animal, yet still beautiful. She was about to make a sound when a woman approached their table.

"Dear Jessica, the beautiful missing person, I'm glad to find you," the woman said, advancing toward her to give her a kiss on the cheek.

Jessica and Maximilien stood up.

"Hi, Amanda. I'm very glad to see you again too," replied Jessica.

"First of all, let me offer you my condolences. What a terrible thing that happened to your son!"

"Thank you, Amanda. Let me introduce you to Major Maximilien Le Gardeur. Major, Amanda is a childhood friend and the daughter of the owner of Bel Jou."

"Delighted to meet you, madam!"

"The pleasure is mine! Your name has been circulating a lot in town since your arrival."

"I hope it's good news," replied Max.

"Of course, don't worry. But I'm interrupting you, aren't I?" said Amanda, turning to Jessica.

"Not at all, the major was just about to leave, right, Maximilien?" replied Jessica, awaiting his agreement.

"Indeed, I'll let you catch up, ladies," Max said, casting an approving glance at Jessica. "We'll continue our conversation shortly."

"Definitely!" Jessica exclaimed.

"Goodbye, ladies," he said, saluting them before leaving for the lobby of the Bel Jou.

As he called a taxi, Max wondered if Jessica really knew the identity of James' biological father. And would identifying this person actually help solve the connection between the two accidental deaths? An hour later, he was dropped off on the main road, at the crossroads of the small road leading to the *Golden Apple*, because a crowd of young students had blocked access. They had all converged on the inn after school in hopes of seeing Nigel and getting an autograph.

After weaving through the throng of youth, and convincing the security guards at the gate that he was one of the guests staying at the inn, Max finally arrived in the lobby.

It was JJ who was at the front desk.

"Hello, Mr. Le Gardeur!"

"Hello, Josephine, you were right, your boss's arrival is causing quite a stir in town."

"I'm sorry about that. By the way, he instructed me to reduce the daily rate by twenty per cent for all the vacationers at the inn for the duration of their stay."

"A gesture that will be appreciated, I'm sure," Max replied.

"Even though we have a lot of empty rooms in this low season," she added.

Seeing that JJ seemed relatively unoccupied this late afternoon, Maximilien decided to ask her a few questions that could reinforce some of the scenarios resulting from his investigation. He knew that she too, as a finalist in the Miss West Indies beauty pageant, had mingled with the members of the famous Fer de lance trio at the time.

"Can I go back in time and ask you some questions about Charlie Liverpool's accidental death?"

"I have no objection, but if you insinuate that I'm guilty of anything, I'll politely end our conversation."

"Don't worry! I hear you! Did you know him well? You must have been attracted to the athlete, the man, right?" he asked.

"Like all the young women of Saint Lucia, yes, to answer your question."

"However, you had a special connection with the members of the championship cricket team, just like Jessica Charles. You met them at festive events surrounding the beauty pageant and the World Cricket Championship held in the Caribbean."

"And then... What exactly do you want to know?"

"I'm going to ask you my question directly. You are an attractive woman, and you were a beautiful young woman at the time. Did you try to make romantic advances toward Charlie Liverpool?"

JJ hesitated to answer, but she always liked receiving compliments on her beauty from a man. Without revealing it, she had a crush on the major. She pushed her hair back in a feminine gesture and, feigning shyness, confided in her interlocutor:

"I'll be honest with you; I tried everything with Charlie, making advances without ever getting any reaction from him, a smiling look, a message of appreciation... Nothing. I concluded that he wasn't interested in girls. Plus, later on, Jessica confided in me that she had a crush on him. So, I definitely gave up out of friendship for her. As for Nigel, he only had eyes for Jessica," she concluded nostalgically.

Maximilien offered her an empathetic look. At the same time, his phone rang, it was Peter.

"Do you mind?" he asked JJ.

"Go ahead."

"Hi, Peter!"

"..."

"What? Are you serious?"

"..."

"I would like to go back as soon as possible. Was it Willie who made the discovery?"

"..."

"OK, I'll be ready tomorrow at dawn."

Maximilien turned to Josephine.

"We found Charlie Roy... He was found dead, hanging from a beam at the reptile preservation agency in Saint Lucia."

Chapter 08

Friday, May 13, 2005

Maximilien was ready and waiting impatiently in the inn's foyer. He had received several text messages from Peter, who had spent part of the previous evening at the preservation agency with Commander Simpson and another colleague from the police station.

He now knew that since his escape from the inn on the night of Danny Ford's attack on him, Charlie Roy had been hiding at the preservation agency. Willie Norris was an accomplice to this secrecy. Even though he knew where Roy was hiding, Willie was not involved in his death, at least according to his statement. It was indeed a suicide.

Peter arrived at eight o'clock. It was easy for him to access the *Golden Apple Inn* because Nigel Glenwood's idolatrous followers were not yet present. Curiously, instead of parking in a way that would allow Maximilien to join him in his car, Peter parked in the parking lot. He got out and walked toward Max.

"Change of plan?" Max asked.

"In a way... Let's have coffee at the restaurant," replied Peter.

They sat down, and Max ordered two coffees. Peter seemed uncomfortable. Maximilien gave him a look signaling him to speak up.

"Commander Simpson doesn't want to give you access to

the agency and has ordered me to no longer cooperate with you, to not assist you in your investigation," he let out.

"Commander Simpson..." Max sighed.

"I'm sorry," Peter added.

"Don't be, you have to listen to your supervisor. Can I ask you one last favor?"

"Certainly, if it doesn't go against my orders," Peter responded.

"Don't worry, I'd like you to drop me off at the chief coroner's office when you return to town. Do you know his address?"

"Yes, his office is near the main market in town."

"Perfect. Now, tell me everything I should know about the discovery of Charlie Roy's body."

Peter shared the information obtained during their visit to the agency the day before. He described the crime scene as they found it and revealed the key points of Willie Norris' testimony.

***

Peter dropped Max off in front of Albert Monfils' office. The building was in the same block as the public market. It was quiet at the market on this Friday morning, as no cruise ship had anchored at dawn. Eighty per cent of the public vendor's income came from cruise passenger's purchases.

Max entered the building and immediately spotted a sign indicating that the chief coroner's office was on the second floor. He went up and saw a young man at the reception desk.

"Hello, how can I help you?" he asked Maximilien.

"I would like to see Mr. Albert Monfils. Is he in the office today?"

"Do you have an appointment?" the receptionist asked.

"No, but it's urgent that I meet him. He authorized me to come see him in case of a problem in my investigation," he mentioned without introducing himself.

"He is in the office today, but I don't expect him for at least an hour."

The young man asked for his name, suggested he wait in the lobby, and assured him that he would contact the chief coroner to let him know of his visit. Max left the office, but since he had not eaten breakfast, he decided to take a stroll around the market.

He wandered through the different sections and quickly realized that Castries' market was divided into four areas; the food market, the artisan shops, the clothing stalls, and the restaurants. A sign caught his attention. It read: Black pudding and eggs breakfast 10 East Caribbean dollars. He approached the stand where a cook, with her back turned to him, was busy with her pots.

"Excuse me, ma'am. Is it too late for breakfast?"

The woman turned around slowly and gave him a surprised look. Where did this stranger come from? she seemed to be thinking. Maximilien didn't give her time to respond and continued, "What is black pudding?"

"It's Creole blood sausage. Do you want some breakfast?" she asked, glancing at the sign.

"Sure, with a good coffee," he said, unsure if he wanted to eat blood sausage.

He sat on one of the stools. After a few minutes, the dish was placed in front of him. The eggs were cooked as instructed, but Max was perplexed by the sausage-shaped blood pudding. He felt it and noticed that one end was tied and the other was open.

"You suck it to extract the pudding from the casing," she said, noticing his hesitation.

"Okay, but can I ask what the ingredients are?" he said.

"It's the recipe for French blood sausage with suet and spices," she replied.

He tasted it and was pleasantly surprised. Max devoured his breakfast. He was about to finish his meal when the young man from the chief coroner's office arrived on the scene.

"Ah, finally, I found you. Mr. Monfils has arrived and asked me to come get you," he said, a little out of breath.

Max paid his bill and thanked the cook, telling her he enjoyed the taste of the blood sausage. He followed the young man and was immediately led to Albert Monfils' office.

Maximilien was surprised by the decor and order in the room. The walls were painted in old pink, and the vintage art deco furniture did not match the occupant's functions. Albert was sitting at his desk, on the phone. Behind him was a painting by Paul Gauguin. He motioned for Max to take a seat by pointing to a chair.

Of average height, slim, with short almost shaved hair, Monfils wore a linen suit in earth color with a shirt decorated with white and blue stripes. A pale blue handkerchief protruded from his vest pocket.

"I apologize; I had to finish this call. How are you?" he asked, getting up to shake Max's hand.

"Very well, thank you, and you?" Max replied, also standing up to accept the handshake.

"In shape! What brings you here?" he asked.

"I'm here to ask for your help," Max said simply.

"I'm listening."

Maximilien revealed that Commander Simpson had banned him from accessing the preservation agency and from questioning Willie Norris, the main witness in the Charlie Roy case. He added that Simpson had ordered Peter Monrose to stop participating in his investigation into the death of James Charles.

The chief coroner had been summoned to the preservation agency the day before; following the discovery of Charlie's hanging body. However, he was not at all aware of the decisions made by Hercule Simpson regarding Major Le Gardeur. This troubled him.

"I will have a conversation with the commander so that he does not interrupt the necessary support for your investigation and allow you to question whoever you deem relevant," he told Max.

"That would be greatly appreciated, but I must confess that in addition to Willie Norris, this includes Danny Ford and Hercule Simpson himself," Max replied.

"I can approve for Danny Ford, but you will not be able to question the commander without presenting irrefutable evidence of obstruction of justice or involvement in any justiciable offense against him," he replied.

"I understand, but I consider him a key witness to two tragic events that have been classified as accidents," Max intervened.

The chief coroner understood that Maximilien was reiterating his theory that there was a link between the dramatic deaths of James Charles and Charlie Liverpool.

"I am listening," he said simply.

"I can provide irrefutable evidence that James's biological father is not Charlie Liverpool," Max began.

He went on to mention that once he had identified James's true biological father, he could begin assembling the puzzle. For this, he needed to gather testimony and facts surrounding the two events.

Maximilien shared with Albert some facts and statements collected since the beginning of his investigation that tended to confirm the link between the two dramatic, accidental deaths. He returned to the objective that young James had when he stayed in Saint Lucia: to know his father and the events that led to his death.

Albert Monfils listened attentively. He mentioned to Max that he was interning in a coroner's office in London at the time of the Charlie Liverpool event but remembered the tragedy that had made headlines even in England. He had taken office in Saint Lucia the following year.

"The attack on me legitimizes my theory. My investigation is upsetting one or more people on the island, just like James's quest, which also bothered them," Max concluded.

Albert informed Maximilien that charges of obstruction of justice had been brought against Willie, but he would not be detained until his appearance before a judge. As for Danny Ford, his request for parole during his investigation had been denied. Commander Simpson had supported this request based on the accused's years of service to the state. However, Ford had, for the moment, been given the chance not to be transferred to the official prison in Saint Lucia, where the conditions of detention were more severe.

"I will communicate with Commander Simpson and contact you later," Albert told him. "However, you will have to give me better arguments to persuade me to reopen the investigation into Charlie Liverpool's death."

"Hoping that you can eliminate the barriers preventing me from continuing my investigation into James's death."

"Leave that to me," Albert Monfils replied.

As he was about to leave the office of the chief coroner, Max threw in one last question.

"Have you ever heard of the character that some islanders call The Mongoose?"

"Yes, but I don't believe in it. At least, as a coroner, I have never received any substantial testimony to that effect," replied the coroner.

***

Once in the street, Max looked at his watch. It was ten thirty a.m. What to do? He decided to return to the inn using public transportation. Since the Castries market served as the terminus for all bus routes, he headed there to inquire.

Thirty minutes later, he was dropped off on the main road and descended the alley leading to the *Golden Apple*. The sun beat down even harder on his head and neck, and the mercury had risen to 32 degrees Celsius. People had started to gather at the gate of the inn. This time, the guard recognized him and stepped forward to facilitate his passage.

He crossed paths with Julietta as he entered the small lobby.

"Hello, Mr. Le Gardeur, how are you today?"

"I'm fine, thank you. I would like to ask you for a favor," he said.

"A favor? What can I do for you?" she asked.

He explained his request to her. She hesitated. Maximilien told her that her gesture could help conclude his investigation into James' mysterious death. Julietta accepted with an embarrassed look. Max gave her more specific instructions on what she should do. She left, assuring him that she would do the task.

Being limited in his movements, Max wondered once again what to do. There were two people with whom he would have liked to have another conversation: Annetta and Nigel's half-brother, Clinton, both residents of Marisule. He went to his room to take a shower and put on a more casual outfit, and began to climb the small alley.

The Mastiff Pitbull announced his presence. Clinton came out to see what was making him bark. He saw Maximilien standing behind the small gated door of the property.

"Rex, calm down!" Clinton shouted as he approached Max. "Hello," he said with little enthusiasm.

"Hello, Mr. Glenwood. I was wondering if you had a few minutes to spare."

Without answering, Clinton opened the door and invited him to sit on a log near the chicken coop. He invited him, displaying a skeptical expression. Despite this, Max was determined to ask him a few questions.

"If you don't mind, I'd like to revisit some points from our conversation the other day," Max said, breaking the silence.

Clinton tensed up as he remembered their agreement. "You promised not to reveal the fact that Nigel is my half-brother," he reminded Max.

"I kept my word, I swear," Max assured him, hoping to ease the tension. "But that's not what I wanted to talk about. I actually wanted to ask you about your mother."

Clinton looked confused and a little wary. "What do you want to know?"

"I saw her at James Charles' funeral and she looked lovely and elegant," Max began. "But then she had a fainting spell and had to leave with Commander Simpson. I hope she's doing all right now…"

"She's fine, you don't have to worry," Clinton answered curtly.

"That's good to hear. And I hope you don't mind me asking, but were you aware of your mother's infidelities, even though your father tolerated them?"

Clinton was uncomfortable with the question, but also strangely provoked by it. It was as if he had never really thought about it before. "My father was a great man," he began, defending him. "He worked hard to provide for us, but he was a man of few words and had a crippling shyness. Everyone looked at my mother, everyone adored her. Every time we went to events, weddings, even funerals, I could see the effect she had on people."

"On men, you mean," Max added.

"Yes, exactly," Clinton replied, pained. "My father didn't deserve that. I hated those men who approached that married woman without restraint."

"And have you forgiven her now?" Max asked, sensing that the conversation was troubling Clinton.

"Of course, she's my mother. I've always had a lot of affection for her," Clinton said bitterly.

Max gave Clinton a few seconds to collect himself before continuing his line of questioning. "Was Commander Simpson one of those suitors?"

Clinton stood up, angry at the question.

"What do you want to know?" he asked. "What are you trying to insinuate?" With that, he concluded the conversation and returned to his house, leaving Max feeling remorseful and somewhat embarrassed for offending him.

Max left the property and was about to head to Annetta's house when he recognized Peter's car coming down the alley leading to the inn. Peter honked to disperse the few fans playing truant in the hopes of seeing their idol. He passed through the gate and parked his car. As he headed toward the reception, he spotted Max passing through the gate.

"Peter, what are you doing here?" he exclaimed, unaware that the orders had already been changed.

"Hello. You were convincing during your visit to the chief coroner. The commander ordered me to resume my activities with you and to make myself available to anyone or any place you deem relevant to your investigation into James Charles and also the attempt on your life."

"That's fantastic. How did the commander communicate this change to you?"

"With little enthusiasm, I must confess."

Both of them shared a knowing laugh. Anticipating that Max would demand to visit the preservation agency and question Willie Norris, Peter had already organized everything in advance before showing up at the inn, as he explained to him.

"Perfect. Give me a few minutes to change my clothes, and I'll be ready to go," said Max.

"No problem. I'll wait for you on the restaurant terrace. A good lemonade would be welcome. They're forecasting over thirty-two degrees this afternoon."

When he arrived in the room, Max found that Julietta had already accomplished her mission. When he returned to see Peter, he asked him if he could make a stop at the airport on the way to deliver a FedEx Express package to the same address as last time.

Twenty minutes later, after the stop in question, they were on the main road leading to the preservation agency. Maximilien confided to Peter the nature of his conversation with the coroner. He took the opportunity to reveal some of the hypotheses he was currently juggling concerning the James Charles case while asking him to keep it a secret.

"Tomorrow, there are three people I'd like to interview; Annetta, Nigel Glenwood, and Commander Simpson," said Max. "And Danny Ford, too. He's still at the police station's prison, right?"

"Yes, I'll organize Danny's interrogation, but it will be more difficult for the commander," replied Peter.

"Just tell him that I want to solicit his expertise."

Peter acquiesced. He asked Max where he stood with James's mother, Jessica. After all, based on the principle that the two fatal accidents were related, she became a very important witness. In turn, Max nodded in agreement.

"She revealed everything to me without telling me everything," he said.

"I don't understand," Peter said.

"I managed to gather the information I was looking for during our conversations. She came to corroborate my assumptions," Max replied.

They began the bumpy ascent toward the agency. When they arrived, Peter parked the car. Willie was not outside to greet them, as he was the last time. Peter comforted Max by telling him he had to comply with his conditions of non-retention and remain available.

"He'll be inside," he said, approaching the door to knock.

On the second knock, Willie opened the door calmly. Upon

seeing him, Max noted that his demeanor had changed, he looked more haggard. He gestured for them to come in.

Under Willie's stunned gaze, Peter began to describe the scene as it was when they discovered the body. While listening to Peter, Maximilien analyzed their host's bodily reactions.

"Here is where he was hiding," said Peter.

"So," Max turned to Willie. "He was present during our first visit."

"Yes," Willie said.

"Was he a friend?"

"Yes."

"Did you offer him this hiding place or did he come to see you?"

"It doesn't matter," he replied.

"Everything matters. I read the preliminary report of your testimony. I am not here today to worsen your situation, but to understand and possibly help you."

Max asked if they could all sit at a table in the center of the large room lined with cages, some glass, others wire mesh, where reptiles of all kinds moved about. He began by asking him questions about these tenants. This had the desired effect, and Willie became more relaxed and spoke proudly of his companions, as he liked to call them.

"Why did you agree to provide the Fer de lance that led to the death of young James Charles?" Max asked, as if throwing a bucket of cold water on a prisoner.

"I never confessed to that," he nervously replied.

"No, but you never denied it."

Willie was caught off guard. He turned to Peter, trying to escape Maximilien's inquisitive gaze, who knew he had opened a door to the truth. Peter only gave him a compassionate look.

"Who asked you to do this?" Max pressed on. "Or rather, who ordered you to do this?"

Willie felt like an animal trapped in a cage. He looked over at the reptiles before speaking.

"I didn't know it was to attack a human," he admitted, crying out loud.

"I believe you, Willie," said Maximilien, placing his hand on his shoulder. "But we need to know the identity of the person who ordered you to provide the Fer de lance."

"Yes, Willie, it could help," added Peter. "Trust us."

"I can't," he replied, sobbing.

Max decided to change the angle of the interrogation.

"Is it because of this person that your friend Charlie took his own life?"

Willie took his face in his hands, feeling more and more trapped.

"Who is this person who torments you? Who is this person who gives you orders, who controls you? Who is this person who caused the death of your friend Charlie?" Max continued louder, as he approached Willie.

"The mongoose," he finally shouted. "The mongoose. I can't stand him, damn him. I hate him."

Chapter 09

Saturday, May 14, 2005

Since waking up on this Saturday morning and even in his dreams from the night before, Maximilien Le Gardeur replayed the virtual audio recording of Willie's testimony in his head. He hadn't divulged the name of the mongoose, but he had provided enough information for Max to identify the person.

Now, Maximilien had a better idea of the context of the events that had taken place over twenty years ago; the world cricket championship, the Miss West Indies beauty contest, and the festivities that followed. And all the protagonists and witnesses from that time were present in Saint Lucia, except for the two Charlie's, the late Charlie Liverpool and Charlie Roy. Josephine Jackson, Willie Norris, Nigel Glenwood, Commander Hercule Simpson, Danny Ford, Charlie Liverpool's parents, and Jessica Charles were all currently in Saint Lucia, over twenty years later.

Willie had talked a lot about the atmosphere and highlights of the championship won by the West Indies team and the famous Fer de lance trio, made up of the only players from Saint Lucia on the international West Indies team. Nigel Glenwood had been named captain a few months earlier. He and Charlie Liverpool formed the most prolific offensive batting duo of all time, known as the runners, as they produced runs by the ton. Nigel often filled the role of pitcher when his team was on the field to ensure the defense. His prowess in this role had made him famous.

Charlie was the most complete athlete, the most self-effacing, and the most gentlemanly in the purest British tradition. Danny was the scapegoat of the Fer de lance trio, chosen only as a defender. But since he came from Saint Lucia, he was Nigel and Hercule's protégé.

Charlie Roy was not officially part of the equipment management team, but he was always around the team. He was the go-for of Hercule Simpson, the assistant coach.

Willie had also referred to the head coach of the championship-winning West Indies team, a certain Timothy Collins, a Briton nicknamed Tim. According to Willie, he had retired on the island of Saint Vincent, which was fifteen minutes away by air from Saint Lucia or forty minutes by sea. Maximilien would speak with Peter, as a conversation with this character could be interesting.

It had been agreed with Peter the day before that the official accusations regarding his indirect involvement in James Charles's murder and the assassination attempt on Maximilien would wait, since Willie was already on parole pending his appearance in court.

Maximilien was approaching the truth, but the motive behind all these dramas remained unclear.

He freshened up and headed to the restaurant. Annetta was present; he heard her humming in the kitchen. He took a seat. He had been waiting for a few minutes, and finally decided to walk into the kitchen.

"Good morning," he said.

"Oh, you scared me," she exclaimed, startled as she turned to face Max.

"I apologize," he said.

The kitchen was small and narrow, with only enough space for two people to work at the same time. This meant a lot of preparation was required during high season. The smell of warm bakes wafted into his nostrils.

"It's a small workspace. Is this where you prepare your famous Creole fish cakes?" he asked.

"Ah! You like them? No, I prepare them at home, like most of the dishes on the menu. As I mentioned before, I have a small catering business at my residence. You should come visit me," she said.

"I intended to do so several times in the past few days, but circumstances prevented me from doing so," he said.

"Would you like to have breakfast?" Annetta asked.

"Yes, but before that, I have a few questions for you, if you don't mind," he said.

"Go ahead," she said candidly.

"In our last conversation, you referred to a great mystery at the time concerning the mysterious death of Charlie Liverpool and the sudden disappearance of Jessica Charles," he began. "What do you remember about these two events and do you believe they were connected?"

"Ah, your question is complicated," she said thoughtfully, placing her hand on her chin.

Annetta took a few seconds to think. She made a nodding motion with her head, looking up as if delving into her memory. She began by talking about the beauty contest. She remembered all the marketing that surrounded the competition, the excitement in Castries because two Saint Lucian girls were finalists. At the same time, there was the World Cup cricket championship. It was an international competition, the West

Indies versus England. The famous trio Fer de lance was on the team at that time.

When the two events concluded almost simultaneously, with Jessica Charles being crowned and the unexpected victory of the West Indies, there was euphoria in town. A few days later, Castries was preparing to receive its champions, the three Saint Lucians. A big celebration was organized on the public square, and it was the perfect occasion to celebrate Jessica's coronation with her runner-up, Josephine.

"You can imagine the atmosphere," Annetta continued. "Unfortunately, some revelers took advantage of the situation and vandalized some businesses, and the police authorities lost control."

Two days later, Charlie's disappearance was reported, and when his body was found three days later, it was like a cold shower had swept across the whole island.

"That put an end to the festivities," Annetta remembered. "The accident theory gradually became accepted. But when Jessica Charles disappeared a few weeks later, all sorts of rumors started to circulate."

"Do you mean that the accident theory of Charlie was being questioned?" Maximilien asked.

"Yes, because during all the festivities, they were always seen together, Nigel, Jessica, Charlie, and Josephine, like lovers. Following his disappearance, we imagined that we would eventually announce the discovery of Jessica's corpse," replied Annetta.

"And..."

"All of that dissipated quietly, as both Charlie's and Jessica's parents maintained complete silence. Gradually, everyone returned to their daily concerns, and normal life resumed."

Annetta breathed deeply, as if she was exhausted. Maximilien didn't dare to question her any longer.

"Come on, out of my kitchen. Go sit down, and I'll bring you a half-honeyed grapefruit and my famous fish cake," she ordered him.

Maximilien obeyed. After devouring his breakfast, he went straight out to the gardens.

***

"Danny, wake up."

"What's going on?" He reacted, sitting up and recognizing his interlocutor.

"Lower your voice, idiot. The investigator is coming to question you soon."

"No, I don't want to," he replied, lying back down.

"You don't have a choice. Don't forget the file I have on you. I'm sure you don't want certain information leaking and circulating in town, that certain of your tendencies become known," his interlocutor whispered, with both hands on the cell bars.

"You—"

"Shut up and think about what you're going to tell him."

***

Outside, Maximilien spotted Nigel in conversation with the gardener, Oscar. They were under the enormous breadfruit tree. The tree was at least twenty-five meters tall. Nigel seemed to be pointing to branches while giving instructions to his gardener.

Max decided to join them.

"It's huge," he said to show his presence.

"Ah, Monsieur Le Gardeur," Nigel said, turning around. "It's not fully mature yet, it can grow up to thirty meters and more at its maximum height."

"Really? And these big green balls are they edible?"

"Very edible, fried, boiled, or mashed, they go well with all dishes. It's the first tree that Oscar planted on the inn's property, he's very proud of it," he added, turning to the gardener. "Hey, Oscar, are you proud of your tree?" he asked him in Creole.

Oscar made a face, implying that he didn't feel the need to answer the owner. Nigel continued in Creole before turning to Max.

"You wanted to see me?" he asked him.

"Yes, I want to have a brief conversation with you." he responded.

Nigel led him to the garden bench where they took a seat. Maximilien had chosen the shaded side and turned slightly to face him. After several seconds of silence, Nigel decided to break the tension in a humorous way.

"You're not here for my good looks, are you?" he quipped.

"Would it shock you if I said yes?" Maximilien replied, playing along. "After all, you are a handsome man."

"You're funny, but know that I don't find it amusing," Nigel retorted, annoyed.

Maximilien noticed that his interlocutor was indeed offended, but at the same time, he found the theme interesting. *Don't go there for now*, he thought. Nigel seemed to be getting impatient, so he needed to quickly change the subject.

"Enough with the jokes, I apologize! I wanted to take you back a few years, to the time of your world cricket championship. I hope you don't mind," Max asked politely.

"That depends on the information you're looking for. If it concerns Charlie's death, I'll politely decline," Nigel replied.

"I see... This tragedy, his disappearance, his body found a few days later in Castries Bay, must have been difficult for you. The loss of your childhood companion, your sports brother-in-arms..."

Nigel jumped up and walked over to the breadfruit tree, where he stopped and turned his back to Max. He looked up at the top of the tree and remained there for a few minutes, trying to hold back and conceal his tears. Maximilien said nothing, realizing he had said too much. When Nigel regained his composure, he wiped away his tears with one hand and his forehead with the other while turning around.

"This heat is oppressive," he declared. "Since I've been living in England, my body can't handle it. I don't know about you, but I'm going back inside where it's cool," he concluded, heading toward the inn at a brisk pace, leaving Max stunned and alone on the bench.

After a few moments, he got up and followed him.

He had hurt Nigel, who, not knowing how to express his emotions had chosen to flee. Perhaps, it was also male pride that had pushed him to act that way. Maximilien had no lessons to give anyone about pride.

He entered the lobby. JJ was at the reception. He greeted her and, noticing that she seemed somewhat upset, he approached her.

"Everything okay? You seem to have seen the devil himself," he said.

"I'm fine, just saw Nigel come in, he passed me in a hurry without greeting me, which is not like him as a gentleman," she replied.

"He probably had his reasons, something on his mind..."

"It's true that his departure is scheduled for this Monday," JJ said.

"What? You're telling me he's leaving the island this Monday?" Max repeated, a hint of dismay in his voice.

"Yes, according to the latest instructions he gave me."

Maximilien began to think. He had to conclude his investigation hastily, as he had no legal or judicial recourse to keep Nigel Glenwood on the island. He was the central witness of his most plausible scenario, at least of the synopsis he was about to share regarding the events that had occurred more than twenty years ago.

"Is the dining room at the inn available for lunchtime or early afternoon tomorrow?" he asked JJ.

"Yes, why?" she inquired.

"I would like to reserve it for a meeting. There will be no more than ten people," he replied.

"Okay," she said slowly, perplexed and hesitant about this request.

At the same time, Max received a text from Peter announcing that arrangements had been made for him to interrogate Danny Ford at the Castries police station that afternoon. He confirmed that he had left a message for the commander regarding his request to meet with him after the interrogation, but he had not received confirmation. He ended by mentioning that he would pick him up at half past one.

Max looked at his watch and, turning to JJ, mentioned that he would like her to be present at this meeting, tomorrow, which she dubiously accepted. Now, how to summon the other people? He judged it would be best to give this task to Peter.

For Jessica, he would send a text that would leave her no other choice but to attend. He returned to his room to prepare for his visit to the Castries police station.

Peter arrived as expected at half past one. Immediately in the car, Maximilien shared with him the latest discussions he had had that morning, as well as, his plan for the following day. They discussed the ideal way for the day to unfold and the potential timing for police intervention, if deemed relevant. Peter accepted the mandate to summon the people Max listed.

"You'll have to notify the chief coroner. As you know, I've already had a discussion with him," Max said.

"Yes, and I'll inform him of the latest findings from your investigation," Peter replied.

"Oh, and do you remember when Willie referred to the head coach of the West Indies team, Timothy Collins? Do you think you can find his phone number?"

"I'll try to get it."

They arrived at the police station at two o'clock. Danny was already in the interrogation room, handcuffed and watched by two policemen. His eyes were swollen from lack of sleep. Despite the context, the atmosphere was friendly due to the professional proximity that existed between the three men. But everyone changed their attitude upon the arrival of the captain and the investigator; the policemen straightened up, and the prisoner lowered his head.

"You can leave us alone now," Peter said to the two policemen as soon as they entered the room.

Maximilien greeted them with a small smile as they left and sat down at the table opposite Danny. Peter took his place next to him. Max said nothing for long seconds, just staring at the prisoner, knowing he had been silent as a fish since his arrest. After more than a minute, Danny began to occasionally raise his eyes to his two examiners, signifying his discomfort with the silence. Max did not flinch. He felt more and more uncomfortable. And then, unable to take it anymore, the man blurted out, "What do you want from me?" Danny asked.

"I am glad to see that you can speak," Max replied simply.

"I won't tell you anything, and you won't know anything," Danny continued, exasperated.

"So, I gather that you have something to say, but someone is preventing you or threatening you. Is that correct?" Max asked.

Danny didn't know how to react to this statement. Maximilien perceived weakness and confusion in his eyes. Unsure of what to say, Danny simply lowered his gaze to the ground. Max decided to change his line of questioning. He wanted to take Danny back to the time of the famous Fer de lance trio and the accidental death of his teammate, Charlie.

"You were a world champion cricketer and part of the famous Fer de lance trio of Saint Lucia. Since I arrived here, I have constantly heard about this achievement. You must be very proud. You were welcomed as a national hero," he reminded Danny.

All of this made Danny stir slightly in his chair. He shook his head nonchalantly, and eventually cast a half-glance toward Max, indicating that he understood his seductive game.

"What was it like to be adored by the whole of Saint Lucia?" Max asked him.

This last comment seemed to annoy him, and Max noticed it.

"You were a star, a top athlete," he added.

"Adored, adored, you make me laugh. They didn't adore

me, only Nigel and a little bit of Charlie. In truth, it was Hercule who put a lot of pressure on the head coach to include me in the international team. He wanted to see his famous Saint Lucia trio on the West Indies team," Danny humbly stated.

"You must be very grateful to him," Max continued.

Receiving no response, Maximilien decided to attack.

"Danny Ford, is that why you agreed to introduce a venomous snake into James Charles' room?"

"No… No." Danny cried.

"No, what, Danny? You didn't agree to play this deadly role out of gratitude? Were you forced into it? Answer me, Danny," Max demanded.

Danny collapsed on the table, placed his head on the table and began to sob.

Maximilien calmed down, sat up straight in his chair, and said softly, "You realize that naming the person behind all of this and the reasons that led you to commit this deadly act could alleviate your suffering. Are you aware of this?"

"Danny, are you ready to reveal this information?" Peter asked him.

While stopping his sobs, Danny remained lying on the table with both hands on his head, making no sound. Max stood up and declared, "Too bad, because tomorrow, the whole truth will be known!" Peter stood up as well, took one last look at Danny, and knocked on the door to let the two police officers know that the interrogation was over.

They left the room, and Peter mentioned to Max that he was going to check if the commander was present.

"Fine, I'll be outside. I need some fresh air," said Max.

Outside, he found a shady spot to sit and reflect. What if he was wrong? What if the scenario he had envisioned about what really happened twenty years ago was completely off? The motives remained very subjective and abstract in his mind. Kinship, protection, love, honor, pride, and greed were the themes he juggled to establish his final scenario. He hesitated. "Come on, Le Gardeur, trust your instincts," he said to himself.

After a few minutes, Peter appeared, looking surprised.

"The commander is waiting for us in his office," he announced to Maximilien.

"Peter, it's better if I go alone," he said apologetically.

"Okay, I understand."

"That being said, you have your work cut out for you. You have to find a way to bring the people identified to the restaurant of the inn tomorrow. For the commander, you can pretend that Nigel asked to meet him and vice versa for Nigel."

"Okay, I accept your strategic proposal. No problem with Willie," he replied.

"The most urgent thing is to go see the chief coroner," Max mentioned. "Don't worry, I'll take a taxi back to the inn."

The two men parted ways. Maximilien returned to the police station. He anticipated his conversation with Hercule Simpson. He was excited and at the same time annoyed, invaded by certain nervousness. He would opt for a roundabout and allusive approach. The young officer at the reception led him to his boss's office.

"Ah, Mr. Investigator, I'm glad to see you again. Come in and have a seat," the commander said in a cheerful tone that Max found exaggerated.

"Liar! Liar!" Jacquot immediately chimed in.

"Thank you for agreeing to meet with me," Max said as he took a seat.

"So, how can I be of assistance?" asked the commander.

"I'm at a dead end with my investigation. I can't seem to put all the pieces of the puzzle together," he confided.

"Perhaps, because there is no puzzle to solve, Mr. Le Gardeur," Hercule alleged with satisfaction.

"You're probably right, but what should I tell Mrs. Charles? I have to give her an investigation report on the death of her son."

"Tell her the truth. It was a tragic accident," Hercule replied.

Maximilien realized that his interlocutor was pretending to sympathize with him while also smiling with satisfaction. Hercule appreciated the outcome toward which Max seemed to be headed. He was lying and, furthermore, he made no reference to the attack against him or the undeniable link to the circumstances that led to young James' death.

"Do you have any children, commander?" Max suddenly asked.

"Uh... No," Hercule hesitated to answer.

"Liar! Liar!" Jacquot immediately shouted.

"Would you please be quiet, you jinx! Excuse him, Monsieur Le Gardeur."

"Being a parent is a big commitment. You always feel responsible for your children's actions, always wanting to protect them, sometimes at the expense of others," Maximilien continued, trying to explain his point to Hercule.

Hercule, trying to understand Max's words, was starting to get annoyed by the conversation. He was about to end the interview, but Maximilien went on.

"You know, I failed as a parent. At least, according to the judgment people have of me. But now, like a light at the end of the tunnel, I'm going to be a grandfather," he added.

"Monsieur Le Gardeur, I'm happy for you, but I don't see how your need to express your feelings and parental guilt fit into your investigation," Hercule replied.

"You may be right again. I'm getting off track. Please excuse me," he eventually admitted.

"I have to leave for an engagement. Is Peter waiting to drive you back?" the commander asked.

"No, but it's fine. I'll take a taxi. Thank you."

And so the interview ended. Maximilien wondered if it had all been worth it. Later, while he was on his way back to the hotel in a taxi, he received a text from Peter informing him that he had been unable to identify Timothy Collins' phone number. *It doesn't matter*, he thought to himself. He replied by texting, "Okay, thank you. Keep me updated on your progress for tomorrow."

He arrived at the small road leading to the inn, and as expected, there was a gathering at the gate. The taxi driver asked if he could drop him off near the main road to avoid the fanatics, to which he agreed.

He arrived at the inn and saw Amanda at the reception desk, she greeted him. As he was about to head toward his room, she stopped him.

"Oh, yes! Monsieur Le Gardeur, Joséphine wanted to know if we should prepare a snack or something to drink for your meeting tomorrow," she asked.

Maximilien didn't want the meeting to be known so openly, but he realized it was too late. *It doesn't matter*, he thought to himself.

"That's very kind of you, but there's no need to prepare anything," he replied.

He continued on his way to his room to change for the

evening meal. "Ah, I haven't sent the text to Jessica yet," he remembered. He picked up his phone and typed a message saying that she needed to come to the *Golden Apple Inn* tomorrow at one o'clock, that her presence was imperative, and that he would provide the reasons for the meeting when he saw her. He asked her to confirm the receipt of the message and her presence for tomorrow.

When Max arrived at the dining room, he was surprised not to hear Annetta humming; instead, there was soft rock music coming from the kitchen. He understood when Justin came out from the back, surprised to see a lodger waiting for his meal.

"Good evening, Mr. Le Gardeur. I hope you haven't been waiting too long," Justin said.

"No, I just arrived," Max replied.

"I apologize for the music. I'll turn off the radio as soon as I go back to the kitchen. With Annetta away, there's only one item on the menu tonight," Justin said.

"And what is that dish?" Max asked.

"Pan-fried white fish served with plantain mash and beans," Justin replied.

"That's fine with me. Can I ask you a question about young James?"

"Yes, if I can answer it."

"You mentioned during our first meeting that you often offered to take young James somewhere, but he declined most of the time, except for the building that houses the Saint Lucia Civil Registry. Would he have mentioned the Castries police station as one of those destinations, by any chance?" Max asked.

"Let me try to remember... Yes, indeed... he asked me for directions on how to get there," Justin replied.

"Thank you!"

After finishing his meal, Max was on his way back to his room when Amanda called out to him.

"Mr. Le Gardeur, we just received an internet telegram for you. Here it is."

Maximilien took the paper, on which he saw the sender's name. The text was short, but what caught his attention were the words: "POSITIVE DNA CONFIRMATION, formal."

Chapter 10

Sunday, May 15, 2005

Maximilien woke up and looked out the window to see a cloudy day. The night before, he had noticed a starry sky, which made him believe that the weather would be clear and sunny. That night, as he savored a good Romeo y Julieta cigar, the upcoming meeting had occupied all his thoughts.

Max had received a text from Jessica confirming her presence at the *Golden Apple Inn*. He also had a phone conversation with Peter, who detailed how he managed to ensure the presence of Nigel and Commander Hercule Simpson. "Well done!" he had said. With the presence of Willie Norris and Josephine Jackson, everyone will be there.

He had scripted the unfolding of this meeting in his head, the order in which he would reveal what had really happened twenty years ago, and the connection between the two accidental deaths of Charlie Liverpool and young James Charles. He would also address the issue of the accusations that would follow.

He finished getting ready and headed to the dining room for breakfast. It was nine o'clock. He walked out through his patio door overlooking the garden of small flowering trees and shrubs. To his surprise, he saw Oscar the gardener trimming bushes on a Sunday!

"Good morning, aren't you off today?" he asked.

"I work as needed. The bushes need to be pruned before the next blooming," replied Oscar, casting a look that indicated he didn't have to justify his work schedule to a stranger.

Maximilien was somewhat surprised by this response. He didn't want to reproach him for his professional diligence. After all, the gardens of the inn were his little ones.

"You were right about the Kravat," Max told him.

When he didn't react, Max continued, "You know, when you said it was impossible for that snake to end up around the inn by itself."

Oscar turned slowly toward him, emitting a small smirk. To Maximilien's surprise, he replied, "Good luck with the mongoose too!"

He turned back to his work. Max, who was looking at him in astonishment, thought to himself, "Is it possible that this old fox knows everything, even about the upcoming meeting?"

In turn, Maximilien gave a small smile before continuing on to the dining room. He was happy to see Annetta in the kitchen. They chatted a bit, especially about Caribbean cuisine. She shared with him details of her culinary specialties as a caterer, such as her fish cakes, bakes, and various fish dishes served with mashed banana and local vegetables.

"But my reputation is more tied to my fruit cakes," she added.

"A fruit cake... My mother always made them for Christmas," he told her.

"Yes, it's a holiday cake, but mine is so good that people ask for it all year round, even for weddings. I'll make one for you when you return," she offered.

"Can I pack it in my luggage?" he asked. "Won't it be confiscated at customs?"

"No, it's an accepted item, don't worry. Plus, I'll wrap it up so it stays fresh until you arrive in Canada."

It was ten thirty when Max left the dining room. He decided to take a walk down to the coast. He crossed the old chicken coop, abandoned except for a few squatters who had taken up residence there.

He reached the sea, a strong wind blowing and the clouds dissipating slowly. *It's going to be a nice day after all*, he thought.

Jessica was the first to arrive at the inn, at one ten p.m. She was greeted at the reception by Amanda. Always understated but elegant, she introduced herself, "Hello, my name is Jessica Charles and I'm supposed to meet one of your tenants, Maximilien Le Gardeur."

"Yes, hello, Ms. Charles, please follow me," Amanda said, gesturing for her to follow.

She invited Jessica to take a seat at one of the tables in the dining room, as instructed by Maximilien, and left her alone. Shortly after, Nigel entered the room and spotted her.

It had been over twenty years since their eyes had met. The emotion was overwhelming. Her beauty was still intact, she had aged well, that was the first thing he noticed. She was now a woman at the height of her femininity.

"Hi, Jessica, it's strange to see you again after all these years."

"Hi, Nigel, how are you?" she asked, impassive.

He looked at her, and she also maintained her gaze on him. He didn't answer. Instead, he started by offering his condolences.

"I'm sorry for what happened to your son. I mean it," he added to make sure she accepted his condolences.

"Thank you."

"I have to admit that I was confused for a long time after you disappeared and I'd like to know why you did it. And I just learned that you were in England all these years. Why didn't you try to contact me?" Nigel asked feverishly.

Jessica didn't answer. Nigel approached her. He wanted to take her in his arms, but deemed the gesture inappropriate. She stood up and decided to share some information.

"It's not because of you that I left the island," she said.

"You left with a tourist, didn't you? You married the father of your child," he retorted with a slightly angry tone before realizing that he was acting inappropriately. "I'm sorry," he immediately added.

"No, that's not what you think... I..." she trailed off.

They heard a door opening. They both turned around and saw Willie enter. There was a moment of confusion, the three of them standing still and looking at each other for several seconds. Willie broke the silence. It had been several years since he had seen them.

"Hi, Nigel! And you, Jessica, how are you?" he asked timidly.

"I'm fine," she answered mechanically. "And you?"

"I'm okay."

"What are you doing here at the inn?" Nigel asked.

"I was summoned by the police authorities."

This answer left Nigel and Jessica perplexed. *What was going on?*, they all thought. Jessica was the first to admit that she had been invited by investigator Maximilien Le Gardeur. Nigel followed suit by declaring that Commander Hercule Simpson wanted to meet him at the inn before his departure.

Joséphine Jackson walked into the room. Jessica and Nigel

realized that she was aware of this meeting and that she too was a participant. JJ had briefly seen Jessica at her son's funeral but had not had the chance to express her sympathy, and her pleasure in seeing her again after all these years.

"I'm glad to see you again and to know that you're still alive after all these years. I heard you live in London now," she said.

"Yes, I'm sorry I left the island without telling my loved ones," Jessica replied.

"I won't ask you why you made that decision, it doesn't matter. But tell me what you were doing in England. Are you married? Where were you living?" JJ asked, firing off questions.

Nigel was attentive, wondering what Jessica would say. However, he would have liked to know why she had made the decision to abruptly drop everything and leave for England.

"No, I'm not married," she began, casting a fleeting glance at Nigel. "I opened two Health Spa shops, it kept me very busy. I lived in an apartment above one of them, that's where I raised my child," she added with a touch of bitterness.

"I'm sorry for your loss, coming back to your country under these circumstances," JJ said, moving toward her for a frank hug.

All this time, Willie had remained silent in his corner but jumped at the sight of the next guest. Commander Hercule Simpson made his entrance. Taking a look at the people present, he immediately felt that something fishy was going on. He addressed Nigel.

"Nigel, did you want to see me?" he asked with a suspicious look.

"No, I thought it was you who wanted to see me before I

left," he replied.

"You're leaving?" Jessica asked, regretting her comment.

"What's going on? And you, Willie, what are you doing here?" Hercule asked authoritatively.

Willie didn't answer and simply looked away. Hercule approached Nigel while giving a polite nod to Jessica.

"What's happening? Who contacted you and told you that I wanted to see you?" he whispered.

"One of your deputies, a certain Peter Monrose," Nigel replied.

"Ah! That damned Maximilien Le Gardeur," Hercule muttered.

Meanwhile, Maximilien arrived in the doorway of the large patio overlooking the fruit tree garden.

"You're probably wondering why you're all here, and I was wondering what you were all doing twenty years ago," he said to them.

With this laconic comment, he entered the room, sizing them up one by one. He thanked them for their presence and apologized for the deception that had brought them all there. He explained that he wanted to take them on a journey back in time. Immediately, the guests grunted with curiosity and incomprehension.

"Who authorized you to gather us together to discuss the past?" Hercule asked passionately. "I don't care about your speech, you're just a passing investigator, and the sooner you leave the island, the better for the rest of us."

"Shut up and let him speak," Jessica replied sharply.

Hercule glared at her, but she didn't look away. Maximilien felt that he had to intervene before Hercule lost his patience and left the meeting. The time to confront him had not yet come.

"Dear commander, your presence, wisdom, and authority are crucial for what's to come," said Maximilien.

Hercule, not understanding Max's last comment at all, stiffened, looked at all the participants, and finally calmed down. Maximilien continued. He began by establishing the broad lines of the context of the time; the championship, the beauty contest, and the festivities that followed. He could see that everyone was reacting differently to his words.

"Jessica, you were in love with Charlie, weren't you?" he asked.

He didn't let her respond and continued, "You arranged to meet him to express your feelings, but to your surprise, he told you he loved someone else." Jessica shifted in her chair, sitting up straight to show she was ready for what was coming. "And you forced him to reveal the name of this person, who turned out to be a man!"

All eyes turned to her. "Yes, Charlie Liverpool was gay," Max declared.

"I knew it. That's why he resisted all my advances," JJ said.

"You're not the only one in this room who knew," Max added without subtlety.

Looking back at Jessica, Maximilien continued, "To console yourself, without malice or revenge, you went to see this man and decided to let him seduce you and succumb."

Nigel felt the spotlight shifting toward him. He looked at Jessica, and then at Max while trying to maintain his British composure.

"Isn't it true, Nigel, that later on, either the next day or the day after, Charlie, having confessed his homosexuality to Jessica, arranged to meet you at the promontory of the secret cove?"

The tension was increasing. Max could see that the commander was giving him a disapproving look, and Nigel was attentive but fearful.

"Isn't it true that he confessed his physical love for you which he had been hiding since childhood?" Nigel was struggling to catch his breath. "Isn't it true that this highly shocked you? And isn't it true that a quarrel between you and Charlie followed?"

Nigel leaned forward and crossed his hands on his legs.

"Isn't it true that it was during this quarrel that Charlie fell off the cliff?"

"It was an accident, it was an accident…" he repeated, starting to sob and putting his head in his hands.

"You don't have to say that, my son," the commander said.

"Your son?" Jessica and JJ said simultaneously.

"Yes, Hercule Simpson is Nigel Glenwood's biological father," Max declared.

Maximilien noticed Willie's reaction, who was clearly unaware. Hercule didn't try to deny it. Nigel repeated several times that it was an accident, that he didn't intend for the fall from the cliffs to happen.

Max approached him and put a hand on his shoulder, saying, "I believe you, it's okay."

"Don't speak any more, you're carried away by emotion. I'll handle this," said Hercule to his son.

"Father, it's the truth. I've been carrying this burden for so many years."

"Yes, Commander, you arranged things for your beloved son. You convinced him not to talk about it to avoid damaging his reputation, even though it was just an accident. And you went to Charlie's parents to convince them it was a suicide and tell them that, out of kindness, you were going to close the investigation by declaring it an accidental death."

"All of this is nonsense, you like to make up stories, my dear investigator," replied the commander.

"All of this to save their honor and that of their son. But we all know that your goal was to silence them to complete your investigation in your own way and make sure that nothing would disturb your son's career, added Maximilien, looking at him with assurance."

"I'm leaving this theater. Come, my son, we have nothing left to do here…"

"I suggest you stay; it will only get more interesting," Max almost ordered him.

Noticing that Jessica was starting to get impatient and wondering where all of this was leading, he moved on to the next act. He asked her to confirm that she left Saint Lucia because she was pregnant and didn't want to subject her parents to the scandal, the dishonor, the birth outside of marriage, and even, potentially, an engagement. Jessica confirmed it, avoiding Nigel's gaze, who seemed to be reflecting on this confession.

Maximilien looked at Jessica to indicate that the rest could be emotionally difficult. She understood and signaled him to continue.

"James Charles, Jessica's son, born in England, was twenty years old when he decided to come and visit Saint Lucia. He wanted to know the country of his parents and his in-laws. But he also wanted to learn more about his biological father and understand the conditions under which he died. He didn't know that Charlie Liverpool wasn't his father.

"In the room, Hercule glared at Maximilien, Nigel was

troubled by the recent statements, Jessica felt the anxiety rising in her, and JJ and Willie were attentive and perplexed spectators.

"For my investigation, I tried to retrace his steps during the two weeks he spent here. This led me to discover things, and I imagine he noticed the same, if not more," Maximilien said.

Turning his gaze toward Hercule, he asked him to share the conversation he had with young James on Thursday, April 21, when he went to visit him to discuss the file of Charlie Liverpool, whom he believed to be his biological father, at that time.

"This is false," he replied, sweeping his angry eyes over everyone in the room.

"No, Hercule, you did indeed meet young James at your office that Thursday. I have evidence, I have witnesses. You even made the activity log at the police station disappear for that day. Peter Monrose confirmed to me that it had disappeared as if by magic," Maximilien said.

"And then, what does that prove?" Hercule responded.

Maximilien paused. He had just made him admit to a first truth. It was time to strike the big blow.

"What does that prove? Well, that you lied about it, that you were aware of the young James' research and findings, that his questioning was disturbing your little world, and that you felt a danger looming," Max replied.

After a few seconds, he continued, "I wasn't in the room during that meeting, but it's possible that young James raised the idea of reopening the investigation into his father's suspicious death. Is that possible, commander?" he asked, while Hercule remained motionless and did not deny anything.

"You decided to eliminate him, you orchestrated his death

with your accomplices who were subjected to your blackmail, and you ordered Danny Ford, Charlie Roy, and Willie Norris to execute your plan," Maximilien said, describing the scenario that led to James Charles' death.

"It was planned for a Sunday because the dining room was closed that day. Charlie, at the reception, knew that the young man would go to get food near the inn. Willie provided the box in which the snake was placed. Charlie monitored the victim's exit, and then went to unlock the patio door of room 11. He notified Danny that the coast was clear. Danny, passing through the garden of small bushes, went to room 11 and slipped the snake inside."

"Willie, tell him he's lying, that he's making up stories," the commander said in his defense.

"Father, tell me this isn't true," Nigel asked incredulously.

"You had agreed with Charlie Roy to inform him, not the poison control center, when the victim realized he had been bitten. You wanted to delay your arrival to ensure that the venom had fully taken effect," Max added. "Things happened differently, but still according to your ultimate goal."

"Willie, Willie, please tell him it's not true," Hercule cried out to him with despair, pretending not to have heard his son's question.

"It's the truth, I participated in it, I'm ashamed," he admitted, turning to Jessica. "I'm sorry; I was forced to do it."

Unable to take it anymore, Jessica got up and charged toward Hercule to strike him.

"You monster, you killed my son, bastard," she screamed.

It was Nigel who stopped her, more to protect her than to prevent her from reaching Hercule.

"Let go of me, you idiot," she shouted, pounding on his

wrists as he held her against her will. "He killed my son... he killed our son!"

Nigel let go calmly, shocked by this declaration. He stepped back, staggering a little, while JJ got up to take Jessica in her arms to comfort her.

"Yes, Nigel, James was your son," Max declared.

Turning to Hercule, he continued, "You are under arrest for the premeditated murder of James Charles, the premeditated attack against myself, and for falsifying an investigation report on the death of Charlie Liverpool. In addition, I denounce you as the mongoose, this character who harassed and blackmailed several individuals on the island to establish your corrupt authority," he concluded.

Nigel challenged his father's gaze, not knowing how to react. Hercule approached him to say, "I did this for you, my son."

It was at that moment, just after this confession, that Peter Monrose and the chief coroner, Albert Monfils, entered. They had been backstage in the rear kitchen during all of these exchanges. Two police officers appeared at the open patio door of the dining room behind Max.

Peter approached Hercule and, with handcuffs in hand, declared, "You're under arrest."

"You have the right to remain silent. If you waive this right, anything you say can and will be used against you in a court of law."

As Peter was about to handcuff him, Hercule, in a fit of rage, shoved him with one hand and sent him tumbling to the ground. He locked eyes with Maximilien, his rage causing froth to begin spilling from his mouth. Charging at Max with all of his six-plus feet and two hundred and twenty-five pounds, he bellowed, "You'll pay for that."

Maximilien realized the two officers behind him wouldn't be able to intervene in time, so he braced himself for the charge. A judo move came to mind, one that involved using the attacker's force against them. As Hercule ferociously closed in on his target, Nigel emerged and tackled him to the ground like a football player.

"That's enough, Father."

Hercule broke down in tears, devoid of strength.

Peter, with the help of the officers, handcuffed him. They were about to do the same for Nigel and Willie when Nigel approached Jessica and kneeled before her.

"I apologize. I had no idea about my father's diabolical plans. You have to believe me…"

She sized him up and offered a small smile of compassion before looking away.

***

That evening, Maximilien was determined to contact his ex-wife, Isabelle, France's mother. He obtained the payphone number from the inn and dialed it, listening to it ring.

"Hello."

"Isabelle, it's me, Max. How are you?"

"I'm fine, thank you, but where are you calling from?"

"I'm on a case in the Caribbean. I found out about France."

"Ah, did she manage to get in touch with you?"

"No, she left a message, but I spoke to Jules for my investigation and that's where I found out about her pregnancy. How is she? When is the baby due?"

"She's doing well. The baby is due around the holidays.

You know, Max, she wanted to let you know, but that doesn't mean she's ready to reconcile with you. I'm sorry."

"I understand, but it's still fantastic news. Congratulations, Grandma!"

"Let's wait until the baby's born before celebrating."

The conversation continued for a few more minutes. Maximilien was happy to have spoken with her. *All in all, an excellent day,* he thought.

***

Monday, May 16, 2005

His return flight was scheduled for Thursday, May 19. That morning, Max had managed to change it to Tuesday, May 17. It pleased him. But before leaving, he wanted to see Jessica and the chief coroner, Albert Monfils. He didn't want to disturb Peter, who was extremely busy due to the events of the previous day. Justin, the driver, agreed to take him into town. First stop, the coroner's office. Maximilien had informed him of his visit.

"Good morning, Mr. Le Gardeur, Mr. Monfils is waiting for you in his office," the young man at the reception told him.

"Thank you," he replied, continuing on his way to the office.

"Come in," Albert said, seeing him appear in the frame of his door.

"Thank you!"

"Congratulations on your professionalism, but it gives us a lot of work," he said, with a mischievous little laugh.

"I'm sorry."

"Don't be, I was joking."

They discussed the next steps. Albert confirmed that Nigel would not be detained until his appearance in court. He did not expect a major sentence in his case. As for Willie, he would face charges of complicity in a crime and attempted murder. His sentence could be as severe as Danny Ford's. As for Commander Hercule Simpson, he could face twenty-five years in prison.

"Since his arrest was announced, I have already received two requests for deposition from people who were blackmailed by Hercule, who had built a case against them. I expect to receive several more in the coming weeks. All of this will play heavily against him in court. He was indeed the mongoose, you were right, my dear sir."

Albert told Maximilien that he would have to come back to testify at the criminal court trial of the commander. The two men parted ways. Max ordered a taxi to the Bel Jou.

Jessica, as elegant as ever, was waiting for him on the hotel terrace. She was sad but happy that the whole truth had come to light.

"Thank you for persevering even though I wasn't completely transparent with you from the beginning."

"You had your reasons," he replied politely. "What are you going to do now?"

"I'm going to stay here for a few weeks and spend time with my parents and friends. But I will return to England, that's where my life is now."

"And Nigel?"

"Nigel…"

"You hid the birth of his son from him all these years."

She didn't answer, and Maximilien changed the subject. They briefly discussed Maximilien's fees and the expenses incurred during his stay. Then, they exchanged kisses on the cheek, and he left.

It was Josephine at the reception desk when he returned to the inn.

"Ah, it's you. You stirred up the cage here," she said jovially.

Maximilien didn't comment but simply gave her a small smile. He told her that he was leaving the next day. Nigel had instructed her to eliminate all expenses related to his stay at the inn. He thanked her, especially on Jessica's behalf. Nigel probably knew that Jessica would eventually have to assume these costs.

"Peter Monrose called for you. He's asking you to call him back," JJ said as Maximilien headed toward his room.

"Thanks, I left my phone in my room. I'll call him from there," he replied.

Upon arriving in his room, he found a small package waiting for him on his bed. The smell quickly revealed that it was the fruit cake that Annetta had promised him. He took his phone and checked Peter's calls and messages.

"My dear Peter, you still have an important task to perform," he joked when he managed to reach him.

"You mean 'my deputy commander,'" Peter replied.

"Ah, I'm not surprised. Congratulations!"

"Interim for now, but it should be official in a few weeks. What is this important task you have for me?" Peter asked.

"I'm not sure I should impose it on you, given your new responsibilities. But I was wondering if I could count on you to drive me to the Vieux-Fort airport tomorrow. My flight is at—"

"You're kidding, it would be my pleasure."

Table of Contents

Foreword 13
Chapter 1 16
Chapter 2 32
Chapter 3 50
Chapter 4 65
Chapter 5 84
Chapter 06 103
Chapter 07 118
Chapter 08 133
Chapter 09 146
Chapter 10 162

References

St. Lucia Historic Sites (Published in 1975) by Robert J. Devaux

National Archives Saint Lucia, Clarke Avenue, St. Lucia

St. Lucia National Librairy, Clarke Avenue, St. Lucia

Organisation mondiale de la santé – Revue Neuropsychopharmacology publiée à la mi-mars 2022.